BIG DOG

BURNING BASTARDS MC
BOOK 1

BY RYDER DANE

ISBN-10# 1-945012-02-1
ISBN-13# 978-1-945012-02-0

Edited by Vinvatar Publishing

Artwork by Jess Buffett Graphic Designs

Published by Vinvatar Publishing
Website: Vinvatar.com

Table of Contents

Chapter One

Future was finishing her set on stage in the bar when three of the biggest men she'd seen in ages walked in. They looked around and walked to the bar to place their orders. From the way the room got quiet when they walked in, she knew the patrons were waiting for trouble to begin.

Her audience was lost before her music signaled the end of her dance, so she slid her feet back into the four inch heels and stomped to the bar. The skintight body stocking she wore drew admiring stares as she walked by the men in the bar. She grabbed the short barely-cover-my-ass skirt from the back of one of the barstools, and wrapped it around her waist, before lifting the hinged counter and walking behind the long, wooden bar. She didn't normally pole dance, but when employees don't show up, the Boss had better be willing to step in and do the job, or else. Kendal was one of the bartenders tonight, and she was becoming flustered. She walked over to where the three roughly dressed men had the little woman standing.

"Hey, Kendal, there's customers waiting, and you can't stand around flirting with good looking bikers without starting a riot with your fan club over there. It's about time for your set anyway, I'll take care of these guys for you." She smiled at the younger girl to let her know she was trying to help her, and she was rewarded with a tentative smile and shoulder shrug.

"I'm sorry, Future. I would appreciate it if you could help these gentlemen. They want to know where we have stashed the Oracle. I don't know what they're talking about, do you?" Kendal backed away and almost ran into the other girl slinging beer down the bar to a customer.

The three men looked even more dangerous than they did scary. They didn't appear to be related, except by the colors they were showing on the back of their leather vests. "So, boys, now that you've scared the daylights out of her, what can I get for you?"

The man with the three day old beard and shaggy dark brown hair scowled at her but tried to keep his temper in check. She knew men like these, she wasn't going to burst into tears when one of them frowned at her. If she showed these men weakness, they would walk over her. She kept a polite smile in place, when she really wanted to lock the doors and hide in her closet. The Burning Bastards MC were a group she couldn't trust. They'd betrayed her once, and she didn't plan to allow it to happen a second time.

"We offer a wide variety of beer and wine is red or white. We have three whiskies for you to choose from, and we carry a lot of soda. So what's your drink?"

Mr. Tall, dark, and scary rolled his eyes at her, *actually rolled his eyes*. She wanted to laugh until he reached into the front of his jeans and pulled out a fat roll of money. He counted out five one hundred dollar bills and put the rest back in his pocket. His big hand slapped down on the cash and pushed it her way on the bar, keeping his fingers on the bills. "Like the girl said, we're looking for the Oracle; you have it—we want it. It's as simple as that. Nobody's trying to scare the girl, and we aren't here to cause trouble."

Oh yeah, this guy had the voice to match the looks. It was a damn shame she was about to piss him off. It was probably the best, though, she had a soft spot for men who looked and acted like he did, and they had both been pricked. It was better to get it over with and move on with the night. She leaned onto the bar with her ample breasts cradled over her folded arms, and looked up at him and his companions.

"Mr., if I had an Oracle, do you think I'd be here in this place, pole dancing and slinging beer to a bunch of drunk bikers and rednecks? I don't know where you got your information, but I haven't got shit that I haven't worked my ass off for. I don't have your Oracle. I told you, I have beer, wine, and whiskey." Just for shits and giggles, she threw in, "I'm afraid you boys are in the wrong place, I'm not sure where the Hobbit village is, but if you Google it, it should come up. They might have one." She turned to walk away, and a hand snagged her ponytail to stop her from leaving.

Dammit, she knew better than to taunt guys like these, she turned back to see the grim looks sent her way by all three men. "All right, I apologize, but you have to admit, it's not every day someone comes in here and demands something that sounds like it came from a movie."

The hand holding her hair pulled her closer, and his other hand tucked the bills he'd placed on the bar into her bra. "We'll be back around later on, sweet cheeks, you keep that attitude, I like attitude. In the meantime, look around for the Oracle. We know it's here, and we aren't leaving town without it." One of his fingers brushed her nipple as he moved his hand from her bra top. He let go of his hold on her hair, and she hated the knowledge that she was disappointed when he let go.

She had to shake herself a bit and clear her head. He was right; he wouldn't leave without taking the Oracle. Damn, just when she got comfortable thinking she was finally away from her past, they had to come looking for her. It had been this way nearly her entire life, and she was going to put a stop to it this time. She had roots here. She had made a few friends, and she liked her life.

At closing time, she locked the doors and made sure the serving glasses and dishes were put in the dishwasher, and the trashcans had the lids on them in the back storeroom. She learned her lesson about going out at three in the morning by herself, the creeps and lowlifes would love to catch a woman on her own with no protection, and no one around to hear if she had the chance to scream. So John or Wanda could take the trash to the dumpster in back, and do their usual clean up around daylight, so everything would be ready before they opened tonight.

She went into the basement and around the cases of beer and kegs for the taps, to the small panels on the far wall. The left one opened and shut behind her with a simple push of her hand. She walked through the short hallway that was actually a thirty-foot tunnel to go into her home. It had been one of the unknown perks when she bought the place.

The realtor hadn't known about the tunnel; she sold the place to her on the condition she had to take both of the buildings, and it was only after they'd closed the deal that Mr.Brennbury had knocked on her door the day after closing, and showed her the passageway. The place was built in the 1920s and had been a speakeasy during prohibition. The tunnel had been built to sneak some very prominent persons out of the building, on the few occasions the place had been raided. The house wasn't anything fancy, but it was comfortable, and they had left almost all of the furniture with the sale.

The old man had been a second generation owner and was a very nice person. What made him pick her ridiculously low offer for the place and give her terms for a mortgage she couldn't have gotten from a bank, was still a major issue with her. She tried to give a little extra over and above her normal mortgage payments when she could, but he always applied it to the principle. Something odd was going on, but she couldn't afford to be too picky at the time, and he was anxious to leave the state and retire to Arizona.

After a long, hot shower and tossing a load of laundry in the washer, she checked her e-mail and paid a few bills. The bar was a good solid investment, and she was thankful her guides had led her this way. It had been a good night even without the five hundred the biker had stuffed in her bra; tips were good. She locked the cash in the safe and went to bed.

She should have known she wouldn't be able to sleep tonight. Thoughts of the big men coming into her bar, and looking for answers instead of pussy was a novelty. The problem that came with the answers was what they wanted; she wasn't willing to give up again. It surprised her the men didn't appear to realize the Oracle wasn't an object—it was a person—her to be exact. She was born Oracle Madonna Smith.

Her parents were products of the 1960s hippie bikers, her father had serious drug and alcohol problems, and a serious belief in the mysteries of ESP, and fortune telling. Her grandmother or aunt, she couldn't get a straight answer from her parents about who had told them that she was born to see the future.

The reasoning behind this pronouncement was that she was born with a piece of thin membrane covering her eyes. The midwife pulled it off her face at the time, but her parents kept the 'veil' in a plastic baggy and taped it into her baby book. They rejoiced time after time as she grew up, and told them things she saw when she touched someone or something belonging to someone else. It frustrated them the gift of sight didn't work on command, and only worked for certain persons.

They tried to use her as a trick pony at the biker meets, but after telling one of the big hairy leaders of a gang from up north that he smelled funny, like the dead possum they'd passed on the road earlier, she wasn't brought out as a party favor again. The fact his body was found a few days later, bloated and stinking by his own men who were looking for him. Her words had been forgotten or ignored by his group. No one took much stock in her observations about the man.

Except by her father's club, the Burning Bastards MC, they made her parents keep her around the clubhouse, or as her father always called the place, the crib. She became the touchstone of the place, never allowed to be like other kids, and always looked upon with suspicion, and fear.

Before any confrontation, she would be passed from biker to biker and encouraged to talk about them. The hardcore guys refused to touch her, and she understood. A few of them scared the hell out of her too. If she'd told everything she saw, there was no doubt in her mind she would have ended up dead.

She didn't like being treated differently than the other children in the place. The other kids stared at her and some refused to talk to her. The men gave her the nickname of little witch, and it stuck over the years. She had tried to leave and live with her mother's parents for a summer, but within a few weeks, she was brought back into the fold "where she belonged".

She tried marriage, but that was a colossal failure. He was handsome, considered a good catch, and a true badass. He was supposed to be her ticket out of there but found the club kept him happy to keep her around. He became too self-important, and one night his ego got him killed. She was left with a custom Harley that she couldn't ride. The ape hangers, or highway bars, depending on who you talked to, were too high, and the bike was too tall for her to put her toes on the ground to balance. She had five grand in the bank and the money Bert had in his pockets when he died. Bert was cremated, and his ashes were spread down in the compound where the gang had claimed as the playground. She was twenty-two and a widow with no kids at the time.

The playground was a two acre tract of land the guys drove scooters around and practiced maneuvering and wheelies on. It was used for break 'em football games and even picnics. It was a place to let off steam and fuck around. It was also used as a place where trials and in club battles were staged. If someone started shit in the clubhouse, they were forced to take it to the playground. Provided the fight wasn't spontaneous. As volatile as tempers flared most of the time, the playground was seldom used to settle such problems.

She'd been pressured to give the bike to the club, but instead traded it in on a used Heritage softtail for her own use. It was a good trade as far as she was concerned, and gave her some small measure of independence. She loved to ride, and knew it would take a special kind of man to get her on the bitch perch of a bike behind someone again.

She remembered the last day she'd spent with the Burning Bastards. Her father insisted she come with them to a meeting between their club president and his counterpart in a club named Lucifer's Breed from a town four counties away. She hated leaving her ride back at the crib, but her father insisted she ride with him. They were to meet in neutral territory, at a farm where the owner was known to be friendly with bikers. The feeling they were driving into a trap refused to let go of her brain, and she tried to tell the VP what she felt. He was one of the men she never trusted, and sneered at her warning. He'd called her a few names and argued the club was becoming pussy whipped by listening to her. He was going to the meeting, and anyone who took her word against another club that had never been a threat to them before was 'candy assed motherfuckers'.

His, "We're bikers, not fuckin' pussies, and if you let this cunt with her voodoo shit stop you from showing up to the meeting, you're going to be meeting me afterwards, we don't need her shit to fuck with our heads."

The meeting went well, and she'd caught the smug looks Dorsey and his buddy, Krebs, kept giving her as they staggered around the campfires acting like the asses they were. She was one of three bitches who had gone on the trip, the other women were servicing their favorite guys while she sat on her bedroll, waiting for the inevitable.

The bikes came out of nowhere, and the resulting chaos was almost funny to watch. They hadn't believed anyone would attack a group this large, and paid for their carelessness in blood. Historically, bikers used knives as a preferred weapon against other bikers, their attackers were not so honorable. Guns, knives, and tasers were used in this fight, and Oracle moved to the shadows trying to stay out of the line of fire.

Luck wasn't on her side that night. Two of the bikers grabbed her, and even though she fought as hard as she could to avoid them, she was knocked out and dragged into the night with several others who were taken for ransom. She owed that VP a baseball bat to the kneecaps for pushing her into the arms of the enemy while he ran like the chicken shit he was.

Over three long weeks she had been used and abused to a point where she began to antagonize her captors into killing her. She'd found out a lot about herself after her time spent with Lucifer's Breed. She learned she could enjoy sex with two men at the same time, without willingly participating. She learned that sometimes pleasure became more intense with a bite of pain tossed in. She also learned that no matter how strong a person was mentally and physically, they could break. They could be brought to a point where they no longer cared what happened to their bodies, they only wanted the end. As they used her body and wished they would just end her, she thought about life after this if she survived. Would she ever be herself again? She very much doubted it. Happiness and everything she dreamed of as she was growing up had moved out of reach for her.

To this day she couldn't explain what had come over her when the man they called Jarl had dragged her by the collar and chain they kept her leashed to a hook on the wall with, and taken her to a room with two other men. They laughed as they pierced her nipples and she screamed. They laughed as they pierced her clit, and she screamed. They laughed as each man forced her to suck their cocks and then bathed her body in their semen. Jarl laughed as he beat her with his thick leather belt, stripping her ass and enjoying the sight of the belt curling around her stomach biting into the tender flesh. She had egged them on, taunting them as soon as she stopped screaming.

One of the men decided that she needed a souvenir of that night, and started a fire in a trashcan to heat up a makeshift branding iron. While they waited for the fire to get hot enough, they took the collar off her neck to have a nice visible spot to burn their brand into her skin for all to see. The argument began when they decided to fuck her in each hole, gangbang style, and have the man with the largest dick take her in the ass, so if they wanted to go back for more, no one had to fuck a sloppy hole. The fight began between Jarl and a redheaded giant called Mule. They each claimed to have the largest prick and during the fistfight to decide the issue, the trashcan was knocked over with no one paying attention to it. Within minutes, the old dried wood of the room's walls was engulfed in fire. A beam fell on top of the two fighters, and the screams of pain coming from them was music to her ears...

She remembered laughing and enjoying their screams. That was all she remembered from that night. How she ended up in the woods with only a blanket covering her naked body still puzzled her. Her eyes were so swollen that she could barely see through the slits when she forced them open. Breathing was painful, and movement was almost impossible. She ended up crawling on her hands and knees trying to find help. She didn't remember the farmer who found her on a country back road, or the ambulance ride to the hospital.

Chapter Two

They waited outside for her to come out after closing time. She never showed, and they decided she must be living at the bar. Maybe she had quarters in the back, or possibly the place had an apartment in the basement, they had no idea, all they did know is that she never walked out the doors of the place that night

They went to a chain, no tell motel near the highway a few miles out of town and crashed for the night. It had been a long ride to this Podunk town and they'd been on the road for almost two days, chasing the mysterious 'Oracle' they were sent to collect.

The only bright spot during the trip had been meeting the woman at the bar last night, at least as far as Demon aka Nail Faultersak, was concerned. She was short, but leggy and those heels she wore while dancing for tips still only brought her up to his chest in height, so he estimated her to be five foot six inches or so barefoot. He still remembered the soft skin of her breast as he'd deliberately touched her when he put the money in her bra. Her nipples were responsive to his mere touch, and he wanted a piece of that pussy. It was obvious her nips were pierced, and the thought of seeing them with a double end threaded bar connecting them, made his cock wake up and hum. That thick hank of hair he'd held in his fist reminded him that he needed to find a friendly piece of ass to fuck—soon. If he was really lucky, he would sweet talk the woman called Future into getting sweaty with him. It was a damn shame he was in a hurry, or he might stick around and find a way to bring her to her knees with his heavy cock jammed halfway down her throat. For now, he grabbed the hotel bar of soap as he stepped into the shower. If he didn't take care of it now, he wouldn't sleep at all, and he needed a few hours of shuteye.

Lucas George, known as Knight in the club, yelled through the door for him to hurry up. "Some of us need to use the shitter and shower too you know." Fortunately for both of them, Demon had finished painting the shower floor with his jizz and was rinsing it off with pure hot water when Knight started complaining. He wrapped a towel around his waist, and left the bathroom still dripping water from his body.

"Sorry to interrupt, man, but I couldn't sleep. That sassy piece back at the bar has me thinking about how pretty her ass would look with my handprint blazed in red, every time she got smart mouthed. If I get a chance to test her out, I plan to ride that pussy 'til she purrs. She rode that fuckin' pole like she loved it, and she wasn't even naked or close to it." He grinned and shook his head. "I need to get laid, man, when a chick with a body suit, or whatever you call that thing she wore, can make me hard as a fucking stone, it makes me want to peel it off her real slow and fuck her real fast." He walked around Demon and went into the bathroom with the small shaving kit he always carried on road trips.

Crazy Charlie was asleep on the sofa. He hadn't even pulled it out to have a bed to sleep on. No one knew much about the greybeard, but he was a mean fucker, so no one asked him about his past either. There was a reason they called him Crazy Charlie, and Demon had seen the man in action a couple of times, so he knew the name was earned.

When he woke up around eleven, Demon called the Prez to tell him what they were doing, and why it would take another day to get the Oracle from the woman that had it. "She denies knowing about the Oracle, and from what I can see of her and her set up, she doesn't plan to change her mind. It would help if we knew what the damn thing looked like you know. How do we know if she gives us the right thing anyway? Doesn't old Merlin know what he is looking for?" He listened to Big Dog, telling someone to find Merlin's fried ass and bring him to the club.

"We are going to head out and try to make her see reason, if that doesn't work, we go with plan B." He slapped the phone on his thigh before remembering the damn thing was fragile, and checked to make sure he hadn't busted another one. Two weeks ago he'd shelled out over four hundred dollars on the damn new phone to replace the one he broke in a temper.

They stopped on the way to the bar for eats, and wolfed down at the Saturday morning breakfast bar that featured a sign saying it was an all you can eat spread. Demon and Knight ignored the stares they drew from the other patrons in the place. Half of the reason people were staring was the show Crazy Charlie put on for them. He carried two heaping plates to the table and stuffed his mouth full, then chewed the mess with his mouth open for everyone to stare in horror at.

His companions were used to this type of behavior when Charlie got a sugar rush. He'd already emptied the little square holder of sugar packets and demanded more from the girl who snatched the used dishes off the table and almost ran to the kitchen. Some men smoked, Charlie ate sugar straight from the package. While he waited for her to get the courage to come back, he reached behind him to the holder on the table there and emptied that one too. He must have taken a liking to the waitress, because when she came back with a cereal bowl full of sugar packets, and sat them down in front of him, he wiped the grease of his face and hands, and told her to wait a minute. He reached for his wallet on the thick chain and pulled out a fifty and handed it to her. "This is for you, don't go sharing it with those pansy assed motherfuckers in the back either." He nodded at her and she smiled nervously, and nodded back.

The fifty slid into her pocket, not the apron and she came back with coffee refills. When they left she was still smiling and gave them a little finger wave goodbye. "I bet she's already at the table grabbing that twenty you left as a tip." Knight was cynical, but probably right in his assessment.

Charlie opened two sugar packets and emptied them on his tongue, before kicking his hog into a rumbling growl. The other's followed suit, they were ready to get the hunt for this Oracle over with, and be on their way back to the crib.

*****

They were back, she felt them come in before she saw them. It was early in the afternoon, and she wanted to get things organized with Clementine before she went with the bikers. She knew they would find out she was the Oracle they were looking for and if she fought them, she might not get the chance to come back and resume her life here. If she went willingly, then they had to allow her to leave the club when she wished. Whatever they wanted from her, she wasn't playing party tricks anymore, and she planned to tell them that too. The fact Crazy Charlie hadn't recognized her yet was no surprise.

He never spoke to her back in the day, back when he was one of the hardcore biker life type of men, he still wore his old-school colors over his leather too. The denim vest with its cut off sleeves flying his patches and designation in the club, was now replaced with the leather vest newer clubs called their cut. Her father had been one like Charlie, old school and ready to ride. No matter how fucked up they were at the time.

She ignored them until she finished with Clem, and told her to give the rough looking sexy bastards at the end of the bar a message from her in five minutes. "Tell them to be ready to ride, I'll be waiting in the parking lot."

She hated the idea of going back, but every time she'd tried to fight her visions, or ignored their warnings, she had paid dearly. This time she planned to embrace them. The plus side to all this was she could finally put paid to the old nightmares and hopefully some of the pain of her past. She was twenty-seven years old now, and felt as if she'd lived a lifetime already, and was working on life number two. Her sleepless night proved to her that she had no other options but to deal with it now.

She went into the back room and hefted her kit onto her Heritage. The one thing she'd taken with her when she left the hospital, and she would not give it up to ride bitch on another bike for the long trek home. She opened the double doors that faced the parking lot and rolled the bike out before closing the doors and listening for them to lock. She patted the tank and didn't feel in the least bit silly talking to it. "Hey, baby, are you ready to go home? Don't get too happy on the road, we will be back here soon and you will still be as beautiful as the day I bought you." She kicked the starter and revved the motor for a few moments making sure she was firing right, and drove around the backside of her building. The men were just coming out of the door and saw her waiting by their bikes.

Crazy Charlie saw her, stopped in his tracks for a moment, and started laughing. He held his sides, and finally sobered up enough to walk over to her, with the others a few steps behind him.

"I got it now, that black and pussy pink Hog, I remember when you got that one. We thought someone stole it or sold it when you didn't come back with the others. Old Merlin was a fucking wreck, and Muffy refused to believe you were dead. I just figured it out, Future, Oracle, and even the name of this place." He leaned in and clasped his hand onto her shoulder. "Well met, little witch. I can just see old Dorsey's face when he finds out you lived. He's gonna be lucky if someone don't kill him. He came back looking like he'd been slapped by his bitch, when the rest of us looked like we'd been beaten by the schoolyard bully. He told us that you died when one of Lucifer's Breed ran you over. He saw it happen. I got my head scrambled and we lost four people that night. You were one of them. You and Frenchy were the only ones we couldn't account for."

He looked back at the two men he was with and back to her. "After that night we patched over the Chiefs. That's how we got these two and about fifty others. Things have changed since then. You're going to be real surprised when you see what's happened."

She couldn't talk, if she tried, she knew she would bawl like a baby after its momma's teat. She locked arms with Charlie and nodded. She knew the two handsome men wanted an explanation, but she didn't owe them one fucking thing, and until she wanted to talk about it, they could get their information from Charlie. She didn't wait for them, they knew which way home was, and she left them standing on the blacktop as she drove away. It felt good to be going on a run again after the past years of only taking the bike out at night to blow the carbon out of her pipes. The Heritage had rear suspension and it rode like a dream. As soon as she hit the highway, she opened her up and stayed on it until she had to find an exit to get gas and use the bathroom. After filling the tank and grabbing a candy bar and a slushie, she strolled around the parking lot while she finished her snack, and it was back on the road for her.

Demon and Knight were both pissed when they heard Charlie's explanation. "Are you fuckin' kidding me? Why didn't they say this Oracle was a woman? And what does she have to do with that asshole Dorsey?"

"Dorsey swore to the whole club that she was dead. He saw her buy it. You two know we don't leave our dead if we can get them out. He made some big story about trying to get to her but there were too many of them for him to try, and she was dead anyway, so he couldn't save her, he saved himself. I hope Big Dog hasn't told anybody that you found her yet, 'cause if he has, Dorsey will be looking to get to her before she shows up at the crib.

"As for the bike, that flashy bitch sat outside the clubhouse for almost a month. It was gone one night and no one knew what happened to it the next day. I should have recognized her when we walked into this place, but you know my wings are not as strong as they used to be, especially after that night she went missing. She warned us, but that fucker Dorsey cut through what she was saying and challenged us all, calling us pussies and shit." He kept talking while Knight called Big Dog.

"It's too late, Dorsey is nowhere to be found, and he was at the club when you called in earlier, so he knows we found her. Dog has Poppa and Butch looking for him. I'm no Oracle, but my money says he'll either try to discredit her to the club as a rabbit. Or do his damndest to make sure she doesn't get there to talk. He's got a lot to lose if she can

23

prove he lied. Hell, her being alive is proof that he lied."

Chapter Three

They caught up with her just before dark. Knight saw a lone bike taking the next off-ramp and was certain it had to be hers. This woman knew how to ride, that much was certain. Of course with that softtail of hers, the ride was more comfortable than his was. They'd played merry hell finding her ass, but once he heard Charlie telling them her history, he could understand her not trusting anyone, even a veteran member like Charlie. He still wanted to ride her hard and put her up wet, but the question was how to get her from point A to B.

Future knew they would catch up to her. They were hardened bikers and used to road work as far as she could tell. Charlie, if she remembered right, was a mean son-of-a-bitch on any given day. If the fight had scrambled his brains, it must have mellowed him. He was one of the men who refused to have her touch him one time, and she'd never approached him again. The way he clasped her shoulder today, it choked her up. It was a sign of respect, something that had never happened before with any of the men.

She stopped at the small diner sandwiched between two chain fast food joints. The place was clean and bright, and the waitress was prompt and minded her own business, even though it was plain to see that she was curious about a woman wearing leather chaps and a leather bandana on her head. Future wondered what the girl would do if the three men from the club came in and sat in her section. *She'd probably pee her pants*. The thought made her smile. It wasn't very charitable of her to have mean thoughts about someone she didn't know, but something about the woman's perkiness drove her into remembering cheerleaders and high school pep rallies.

She glanced up when the front door opened and the three bikers walked inside. They looked around the place, spied her sitting in the back corner, and headed her way. So much for her relaxing dinner. She sat straighter and gave Charlie a small smile as they pulled out chairs and sat down, surrounding her with a wall of beefy tattooed muscles and scruffy beards. ""Glad you could make it. We were lucky the rain held off most of the day. I sure didn't want to get caught in it."

Charlie looked from one man to the other and then to her. "I forgot to introduce you to these yahoos before, the one with the red hair is Demon, and the one with the brown hair is Knight. They're a couple of pricks, but they're alright." He grinned at the grumpy looking men. "They do double duty as Nomads and enforcers for now. Elections are coming up in a month, and once the dust settles, they will probably be one or the other. Blending the clubs brought its own problems you know."

Future knew what Charlie was talking about. Nomads were the men who traveled between the club's chapters. It was unusual to have two or more in a chapter, let alone just hanging out at the clubhouse. Things must really have changed. The Bastards chapter belonged to the mother chapter, and the last she knew an older biker named Georgie was the chapter's Nomad. At that time they didn't actually have designated enforcers. Every brother in the club kept the peace and the rules.

The waitress slowed her walk as she came around the corner and saw that she had more customers. She turned back and grabbed menus before approaching the table. Once miss perky tits got their orders on her pad, she laid her hands on the two younger men's shoulders and leaned down between them. "I'll be right back with your drinks, boys, not to worry, I know how to take care of thirsty men."

The looks on their faces made Future laugh out loud. Charlie was pouring sugar into his mouth from the canister, and almost choked. The laughter and subsequent flirting by the waitress with the men broke the ice around the table.

Demon started asking questions, trying to fill in the gaps of the story Charlie had told them, and she explained in short to the point answers.

"So, what happened that night to make Dorsey say you were dead? If he hadn't been sure you would never be seen again, he would have needed to have a damn good excuse as to why he didn't help you get away. So what's your version?"

She wasn't going to answer them, and told them so. "I will talk to the Prez, I don't plan on making a circus out of the past." She looked toward the window into the waning light. "If Dorsey is around, I want a baseball bat." She tossed a twenty on the table and stood up to leave. "There is a small motel right around the corner, that's where I'll be for the night. We'll catch up in the morning."

Just for shits and giggles, she had a few words with Miss Perky Tits on her way out the door. "You're wasting your time on those two, it's the old guy you should be concentrating your time on, sweetheart. He's got a bigger dick and is filthy rich. The way to snag his attention is to hand him a baggy full of sugar packets, he eats them like candy." She leaned closer to the woman who was now concentrating her eyes on Charlie. "I saw him give a waitress fifty bucks for a handful of sugar one time. The next morning I saw her stagger out of his hotel room counting a wad of cash, the poor girl was walking bowlegged."

Future was forgotten as the girl dropped to her knees behind the counter and dug around for sugar packets. She wanted to laugh, but waited until she left the building and was on her bike. It felt good to play a small prank on the guys and the woman. Hell, Charlie would tip her well for the sugar, and if he was lucky, he might get a bit more than a sugar rush to sweeten his dreams.

She didn't need to be an Oracle to conjure up their faces when the waitress began ignoring the meatheads, and started working her wiles on Crazy Charlie. She was still grinning as she let herself in the shabby, but clean motel room. She took a long hot bath to melt the kinks out of her ass and thighs. Her shoulders had stopped screaming at her after they went numb several hours ago, but she sank down as low in the deep water as she could to let the heat work its magic in those muscles too. Thankfully the heat did its job and she should be able to finish the ride tomorrow. Knowing she was going back into the world of crazy voluntarily, had to make her as crazy as Charlie.

She wondered what her parents wanted so badly that they got the big guys to track her down. She'd cut all ties and made no effort to contact them after the night she slipped into the compound and rolled the Heritage out through the gate.

The hospital people had been nice, and the cops had done all they could to get information out of her about how she came to be found on the side of that road. She had been consistent with telling them that she had no memory of anything that happened to her before she woke in the hospital. With the extent of her injuries and the burns that had melted the flesh on her back, she'd been in the hospital for almost three weeks. After the first week, the police stopped bugging her every day and only came around twice during the last week she was there.

She'd slipped out of the hospital as soon as she could walk without a walker, or someone near enough to catch her if she fell. Hitchhiking over a hundred and fifty miles brought her a mile from the clubhouse, and she walked the rest of the way. She could have wept if she had the time, when she saw that no one had disturbed her personal stuff in the saddlebags. Her ID, bankcard, and a change of clothes were all she had in the world when she'd left the place. One other thing had been sitting in the bags, and she took it out to stare at the logo of the club on the back. Her colors still advertised the club and the fact it was the mother chapter. Staring at the garment made her decide to wear it on the last leg of her journey home. It was her history, the leather cut she was wearing the night of the attack hadn't been her original one, this denim sleeveless vest was. Old school to say the least, yet it somehow gave her comfort to remember the day she got it. Most women that she knew never wore colors, unless they were like her, a young widow who'd taken on her old man's colors, and had the widow's patch to prove it. The vest had actually been a gift from the old group President. It declared her to be property of the Burning Bastards MC. It didn't give her special privileges, or a voice in the group's activities, it was her protection, her independence from being claimed or molested by unwanted attentions. Shaking her head, she got off the bed and stood up to try it on. It was a little tighter in the chest, but other than that, it fit fine. She took it off and dropped the towel from her body, before slipping between the covers and falling asleep.

Luck was on her side that night. She'd gotten four and a half hours of sleep before the nightmares began haunting her dreams. The searing feel of fire raining on her back and shoulders, and the numbness of her arms from being restrained, bound by ropes and a metal hook, woke her. As far as she knew, she no longer screamed during her nightmares. She couldn't remember what was different about this dream, but it was almost as if she was enjoying what was happening to her. The fear was absent when she woke. That, in itself, was a mixed blessing, because she wasn't certain she would like in reality what her body appeared to like in her dream. She was sweaty and horny and it was probably a good thing Knight and Demon were in a different room than she was, or they would find out the damaged woman was in fact damaged. Her body bore more scars than it was designed to bear, and if the sight of the scars didn't put a man off, her masochistic need to feel pain during sex in order to achieve a satisfactory orgasm—would.

She had tried a year after her body healed. No matter what her partner had tried to give her pleasure by doing, it took her pinching and yanking at her own breasts, while he fucked her, to have a small but welcomed orgasm. She ended up apologizing to the guy while he dressed right away, and told her that she was a great lay, and tight fuck. "You are just too freaky for me, I can dig the scars, but I'm not into dishing out pain, and my dick's not enough to make you happy anyway. I can tell." Sadly, he was right, his dick wasn't very large, but he was damn good with his lips and tongue, and if she wasn't wired as a fucked up mess, he would have been enough to make any woman happy.

She looked at the clock and closed her eyes, willing herself to go back to sleep. Four a.m. was too fucking early to wake up. At four thirty, she gave up and took a quick shower. She put on her jeans and chaps, but instead of her leather jacket, she wore a red wife-beater type of top and pulled her colors on over the top. She braided her hair in a tight rope and packed up her toiletries into the saddlebags, left a five on the pillow, and the key on the dresser. Twenty minutes later, she was back on the highway. Traffic was sparse and she almost laid the bike down when a family of skunks crossed the road in front of her, but luck was with her and she pulled around them before they decided to spray her for scaring them. Thankfully the doe and her fawn waited politely before crossing the road, just before dawn.

*****

Knight stepped out of the hotel room door and saw the pink over black hog was no longer sandwiched between their bikes. It was barely daylight and he'd purposefully set the alarm on his phone to wake them up early so they could get a good start on the day's ride. He knocked on the door next to the one he and Demon had shared, and heard Charlie grumbling and a woman's voice could be heard too. That was still a puzzle to him.

Last night at the diner, the waitress came back to the table and began fawning over the greybeard like he was her long lost soul mate. She brought a sandwich baggie stuffed with sugar packets and leaned over Charlie, to tuck them inside his shirt. Up until then, he had hopes of getting the woman to suck his cock in the parking lot to relieve the hard-on the presence of Future caused with just the sight of her face and those weird eyes she had.

Instead, Charlie told them that he would be taking a room of his own, and not to wait up for him. The old fucker had somehow snagged that pretty piece of snatch out of his and Demon's immediate plans of double teaming her for the night. They often shared women, Knight preferred it himself. Yet she acted like they no longer existed, and from the sounds they'd heard coming through the thin walls, she either faked her orgasms in a loud way, or the old boy had moves no one thought he would have. Listening to them into the wee hours of the night did nothing to make him feel better or alleviate the need for him to relieve his thick cock at three this morning in the shower.

He wasn't the only one the squeals and grunts affected. He'd no sooner left the bathroom than Demon shoved his way past him into the room to take a shower too. That little witch was going to have to pay for this one. He would have her beneath him soon, and when he did, she was going to make up for the hell this trip had caused him. Knowing she was tying him in knots, and he'd never even touched her, was giving him serious doubts about his sanity.

Demon came out of the door holding his kit and tossed Knight's at him. From the squeals and "Oh Daddy's" they heard through the door, they figured it would be awhile before Charlie got his shit together enough to ride. They left a note stuck between the speedometer and ignition on Charlie's '46 Indian Chief. "Going to the diner."

They gassed up their bikes and took their time over a hearty breakfast while waiting for Charlie to show. A few scooters pulled in and the sight of shiny chrome and like new leather jackets gave them a few minutes of amusement. Two of them were full dressers complete with double seats and arm rests for the passenger's comfort. The owners of those turned out to be older couples that enjoyed riding for the fun of it. One even had a stuffed toy hanging between the Tupperware "trunk" and the shiny decoration rail surrounding it. Seeing the old men helping the *old ladies* off their perches made the two men smile. There wasn't anything to laugh about there. It was good the old people spent time together and had fun.

Charlie pulled up, eyed the chrome commandos, and spit on the pavement before parking his bike next to Demon's hog. He stood back and let his passenger get off the bike and she gave him a quick kiss before walking to her car and getting behind the wheel. Charlie headed to the doors of the diner without so much as a backwards glance. The younger men could only stare at him with admiration. The geezer still had skills.

Demon couldn't resist, "I don't suppose you considered sharing the wealth last night or this morning did you? I see how you are." Charlie grinned and nodded his head.

"I saved you boys from being chewed up and swallowed down by that she-wolf. I swear it's been a while since I've let something that wild have at my helpless body." He rubbed his chest. "I got scratches and bite marks to match, and that's just on my chest. If she wasn't such a fancy piece, I'd give her the job of being my old lady."

Charlie ordered a large breakfast and for once didn't put on a show for the onlookers. He finished his coffee, and stood, "Let's collect some miles, boys." He tossed a five on the table and walked to the register to take care of the bill. The nice looking older woman smiled at him and shook her head. "Your bill has been taken care of, the man that paid it noticed the veterans patches on your vests, and told me to tell you thank you."

He looked around and only saw one possible benefactor, it was a couple actually. He looked their way and saw the slight smiles and nods, and he nodded back. He thanked the woman and left the building with his companions right on his heels. That kind of thing happened once in a while, and he appreciated it. Usually it was done by people who had less than he appeared to have, and it made him feel guilty and good at the same time.

Charlie had gotten his nickname while he served in Nam, and it carried over when he left the Army. After a failed marriage and the death of his parents, he'd made the Bastards his home and family.

Knight wanted to tease Charlie about his good fortune on the trip. He was the one that figured out the Oracle mix up, and the one who got laid, now they got a comped meal. Maybe the old man should buy a Lotto ticket and they could all retire on the winnings. Instead, he saddled up and drove out of the lot without words. The one thing you didn't tease a Nam Vet about was his time put in. His old man was the same way.

Chapter Four

It was close to dinnertime when she drove through town, the place hadn't changed much in the past few years. The new fast food place by the highway ramp was about the only new building she'd seen, and even that was taking on a worn down look. She idled her bike at the driveway leading back into the woods where the clubhouse sat, to gather her feelings. The atmosphere seemed to be in a holding pattern, waiting for something or someone to show up and burst the bubble to relieve the pressure that had been building for too long. Something wasn't right here, and she started on the long driveway into her idea of hell.

The gate was two hundred feet down the hard packed sealcoat, and she wasn't surprised to see two Prospects manning the post. The bald headed one scrutinized her from head to toe and took his time looking the Heritage over before allowing her to pass through the chain link the skinny, pimple faced kid was holding open, once he got the nod from his partner. Another two hundred feet and she saw the crib. It had been given a clean coat of paint and the doors were no longer hanging by three leather strips that did duty as hinges. The parking area was also seal coated like the driveway. Seeing a few people milling around outside, and sitting at small tables by the front doors, wasn't a surprise either. She parked her bike in the second row directly in front of the doors.

That weird bubble of anticipation she'd felt at the road burst the minute she walked through the door of the place. There were kids everywhere. She'd walked in on someone's birthday party and one little boy was running around so fast, she almost collided with him as he flew past.

The energy of the place slammed into her and she widened her stance for a moment to take it all in. Several adult women stared at her and a few men were scattered around the room, but no one approached her, so she made her way to the hallway leading deeper into the club, being careful to keep her hands up and away from stray kids forcing her to steady them. She liked kids, the problem was, if she touched them, she read them, and it seldom turned out good. That's why she liked her bar. No heartbreakers there. She might feel sorry for adults if they were ill, or going through a rough spot in their lives, but kids made her cry.

The chubby young man sitting with his feet propped under his chair untangled himself to stand in front of the door. He looked her up and down suggestively, and she cocked an eyebrow at him. "Really? I will turn around and leave the same way I came into this place, and it won't hurt me a bit." She leaned toward him, "If you think you will get away as easily when they find out one of the Bugs turned me away, you can kiss your ass goodbye. Move."

He stared at her for a minute and decided she looked harmless enough. She was a good looking older bitch, but from the looks of her kit, she was genuine. He nodded his head and stepped aside.

She stepped into a new addition to the old clubhouse. The stainless steel furnishings and bar were all modern, and gave the impression of coldness. She didn't like the room, but then she wasn't planning to be a frequent visitor here either. She sat at a table in the corner of the room to observe the people coming and going, from the buffet of pizza and burgers, salads and fruit, to the bar, getting beers and soft drinks. She placed her saddlebags on the chair and walked to the food. She hadn't bothered to stop to eat on the way, and she was hungry and thirsty. The bartender looked at her in puzzlement, but handed her a longneck, which she promptly drank down almost nonstop. When she nodded at him again, he shrugged and set another up for her. That one went back to the table with her and she sat by herself eating and watching the people, half of whom she'd never laid eyes on before.

Charlie told her the other club patched over to the Burning Bastards. Seeing one of the faces that were at the meeting that night made her heart lurch, but he wasn't an enemy. She zeroed in on one of the men that had hung with Dorsey back in the day. He either didn't recognize her, or was ignoring her presence and that was fine with her. There was a small commotion at the door and all eyes watched as the Prospect that had been tending the post skidded on his back a few feet into the room. He was out cold, and she wondered who had the power to hit the Bug hard enough to make him slide that far.

The biggest man she ever saw in her life stomped through the door with Demon, Knight, and Charlie right behind him. He was at least a head taller than Demon, and as wide in the shoulders as his companions. He was handsome in a very rugged way, but the sneer on his lips gave him a cruel look. If they'd met in her bar, she would be enjoying some seriously erotic dreams about this guy. Even in the bar, she would flirt and joke, a man like him was her kind of guy, and she would have to keep her wits about her. He might be her idea of a damn good time, yet she knew he would freak if he saw her scars. He scanned the room until he saw her, and then he crooked his finger in a come here gesture.

She frowned, but decided to humor the behemoth. Snagging up her bags, she hung them over her shoulder, and took her time walking over the span between them. "Yes?" She wasn't about to let him know she was intimidated if she could help it. The rules, remember the rules. You came voluntarily, under your own steam. Unless you break the rules, they can't do a damn thing to you. You owe them nothing. The pep talk helped her strengthen her spine and appear to be relaxed.

"I'm glad to see you could join us, especially after such a long absence. You have some explaining to do, but I want to know what I'm dealing with." He spoke to a man she hadn't noticed come into the room behind the rest of the mountains of muscle. "Donnie, get me the kid." He kept looking down at her and didn't seem to blink.

Donnie came back with the little whirlwind boy that almost ran into her earlier. He looked tired, but he was smiling. "Hey, Big Dog, did you see all the cool stuff I got for my Happy Birthday? I did what you told me to, and said thank you to everyone too."

This was the test, she had a feeling earlier when she saw the kid, but this was going to be much worse, "I don't do kids. I don't do tricks for parties, and I don't like where this is going, so ask me something else."

His eyes narrowed, and he flatly said, "You do kids now. Stop fucking around and do it."

Deep breaths witch, remember? You can do this, just once. Right? She shot him a look of hatred, before dropping to her knees and reaching for the little boy. "Hi, big guy, my name is Future, what's your handle?"

To give the kid his due, he didn't go right to her. He waited for the nod from his idol, Big Dog. He got the nod and stepped into her reach. She tried to brace herself for a sickness, or looming death. What she felt from Kevin was almost worse. The kid had been abused by an authority figure in his life, his mother. She had sold him to a man that hurt him so badly that Big Dog took him from the hospital and brought him here to live. It didn't take much for her to find the answers the big guy wanted to know. She knew who the abuser was, thankfully Kevin had blocked most of his abuse out with the concussion that had landed him in the hospital to begin with.

She pulled back to hold him with her hands on his shoulders, and gave him a wink. "Kevin, I know what you wanted for your birthday, and I think you should have told him what you really wanted. Hang on for a minute and I'll check, okay?" The kid cautiously nodded his head. She knew he thought she was crazy, but that was alright. She stood up and held her hand out to Big Dog.

"Kevin, age five, you found him in St. Mary's almost a year ago. Yes, to all of your suspicions, and more. Kevin wants a question answered that only you can give him, and he is afraid to ask. Will you allow me?"

His scowl became even darker while she spoke. He held out his hand and clasped hers in the palm of his. He certainly didn't like the idea of her possibly knowing his thoughts. She quickly filtered through his brain, until she found the little spot she was looking for and it made her smile. She pulled her hand back and nodded to Kevin.

"Ask him for what you want, kiddo, I bet he says yes."

The little guy had such a look of hope on his face that if she wasn't sure of the outcome, she would be as anxious as the child was. He looked at her, and she nodded again. He took a deep breath, and walked over to his hero. Big Dog tried to look friendly, but the perpetual scowl must be permanently etched into his features, because even when he crouched down to make it easier for the child to talk to him, the look remained.

"I thought you said you wanted the bike for your birthday. You should have asked for something else if you wanted it, little man."

Kevin opened his mouth and closed it, and blurted his request. "I, I want you to be my dad, I don't got one. You're not afraid of nothing, and I like you bester than anyone I know. You won't let anybody hurt me, just like a dad should, so I really wanted you to be my dad for my Happy Birthday." He shrugged his little shoulder and finished with, "That's all right if you don't want to be my dad, I still like you a lot."

The man's head bowed for a moment. He looked at the child's trusting face and braced body. He knew the kid was gearing up for disappointment, but he feared for his ears when he told his nephew that he wanted nothing more than to be his father. If his sister wasn't already dead, he would have given the order himself once he found Kevin's broken little body in the hospital.

"Kevin, look at me." The child's quivering lips remained closed and his brown eyes were dripping with tears, but the little boy looked up. "I want you to know I had the Suits file papers for me to adopt you two months after I got you. Who wouldn't want a kid like you for a son? I'm glad you're not mad at me for jumping the gun and going behind your back like that, but you were mine the day I laid eyes on you." He reached out a hand and laid it against Kevin's cheek. "No one—and I mean no one—is ever going to hurt you like that again. I love you, kid."

While the small gathering increased in size from curious people wanting to know what the child was yelling about, Future went back to her original seat and watched the mini circus. For once her gift had helped the two involved and she felt good about the outcome. Thinking about touching Big Dog, even for the brief time she had, made her shiver. There were spots in his being that she hadn't been able to read. It was refreshing not to have to take on all of his secrets. The kid was right. Big Dog wasn't afraid of much, and the few things he might have feared, she hadn't seen.

She knew she hadn't been summoned here to deal with this family drama. It had been a test of sorts. She texted Clementine to see how the bar was doing and they chatted for a few minutes. All was well at home, and there was a very happy little boy still dancing around the room looking so weary she was afraid he would drop in place from exhaustion. One of the women she'd seen when she came into the front door, swooped Kevin up and tossed him fireman style over her shoulder amidst his calls of goodbye to everyone in the room.

Big Dog stepped into her line of sight and pulled out a chair to sit down at her table. Ah, now the real reason for getting me here.

"You did good with the kid. So now I have a treat for you. You might even call it a gift. Come with me." He stood and walked toward a door near the back of the room and she had to quicken her steps to keep up with his stride. He waited for her at the door and opened it for her to walk through before him. A gesture so polite that she hadn't expected it from him, but she went with it. The short hallway led to steps leading down, and they went down. Another door, and again, she was ushered through first. The room was large. She wasn't surprised to see what appeared to be cell doors like they had in prisons with the tiny windows in the door and bars in the openings.

Demon and Knight were there, along with two other large men, one was bald and sported tattoos on his head where hair should have been, and an earring of thick gold. The other man appeared to follow the fashion of Goth. Everything he wore was black, right down to the three teardrops tattooed under his eye. He was as big as Demon, but much scarier in appearance.

"You know Demon and Knight, the guy in black is Freakshow, and the other man is Seth." He nodded to Freakshow and he opened one of the two cell doors, walked into the room and dragged out a man wearing a Breed cut. He pulled the resisting prisoner over to stand six feet from where she was and grabbed the greasy hair, pulling the man's head back so she could get a good look at him.

Her blood was running fast and hot. He was one of the bastards who grabbed her to begin with. He'd laughed while he violated her body and pounded his fist into her ribs afterwards. He was also one of the men who killed Frenchy.

She bunched her fist and started forward, but Big Dog held her back.

"Tell me who this man is and what he did the night of the attack." He wasn't giving her a choice, if she wanted to hurt the bastard, she was going to have to relive the night, she shook with the need to finally have some payback.

"In fact, let's see who else we have to sweeten the deal for you." Seth opened the next door and she waited to see who he was bringing to the party.

44

Before he had the man completely out of the doorway, she could see that it was Jarl. The cruelest of the bunch who had tortured her. She had scars on her body that reminded her of his cruelty every time she looked in a mirror, and the temptation to kill the evil bastard was too much for her to exercise caution, there was an orange red haze over her brain and she yanked her arm away from Big Dog's grasp, and ran toward her nightmare. She landed a steel-toed boot to his crotch and reached for the knife she carried in a sheath in the other boot. Her hand was yanked up with the knife in her fist, and another arm ringed her waist as she struggled to be allowed to finish the job that should have been done at the birth of the monster.

"I will give anything to kill this cocksucker, anything. Let me have just two minutes, I'll gut him and play in his blood. I'll even clean up the mess. I owe him, I owe him so much pain and hell that you will never know." Seth pulled Jarl's head back and she could see where the evil bastard's face was scarred from the fire the night she was dumped in that field. The scar wasn't anything compared to the ones he'd left on her body, but she rejoiced in seeing that he had suffered, even if it was in a minimal way. She grinned at his startled face as she spoke. Her next kick barely connected to his gut, but watching him double over made her laugh. She screamed as many filthy words as she could think to scream at him. She struggled in the embrace that held her so tightly she had trouble breathing, and she cursed the men who put the prisoners back into their cages.

Knowing she was crying and not giving a damn who saw her tears, she fought her fatigue. "Please, let me have them." Big Dog held her still. He was as bad as the other men she'd known all of her life. To dangle two of her nightmares in the flesh in front of her and then refusing to allow her to finally put an end to them was cruel. She stopped fighting his hold. He was too big, too strong for her to break free. As she came back to herself, she realized there was no way the men in the room would allow a female to do a man's work if she got the chance. He let go of her middle and squeezed her wrist to make her release the knife. "You can break my fucking arm, I'm not giving it up. I'll put it away, but I won't give it up." He released her, and she slowly put the knife back into its sheath.

When she straightened up, she met his steady gaze. "The first one is named Reeker, and the second one is tagged Jarl. You need a blow by blow account? Reeker helped two others beat Frenchy until he passed out, you want the gory details? They hung him by his feet and took turns kicking his head into hamburger. His skull was shattered into little pieces, and they kept kicking. Those fucking animals laughed the entire time. So you think about that, and be happy you weren't forced to watch it happen.

"As for John Doe, I'll be seeing him in hell."

She'd developed a raging headache, and had to get away from the temptation to say fuck it and attack Seth, to get to Jarl. She turned around and headed for the door they'd come in from. On the way through the door, she picked up her bags and started up the stairs. She walked without stopping or hesitating through the large rooms and out of the front door to her bike, got on, and left the compound. She needed a hot bath to take the pain out of her back and relax the muscles that were still tight in her shoulders. There was no way she wanted to have to deal with Merlin and Muffy tonight, so she headed back toward the last town she'd driven through on the way there. They would expect her to stay in town, or with her parents, but that wasn't happening.

She found a small motel near one of the popular lakes and was glad it was the off-season so she could have one of the more isolated cabins. She took the place for a week, assured that she would have as much privacy as she needed.

Gladys was an outgoing woman with a very perceptive aura about her. "Me and Ralph are going to visit my sister for the week, so nobody will be here at all. For all anybody knows, the place is closed for the winter break." She was cheerful without being cloyingly sweet, and when they accidentally touched fingers when she handed over the key to the cabin, they both got a shock. The relieved laughter broke the ice completely, and Gladys came out from behind her desk to give Future a hug. "Now you come to the back, and I'll clean out the fridge a day early, so you can feed that skinny belly of yours."

Gladys loaded her down with food enough to feed her for the week, and helped by hauling the groceries in the box behind the driver's seat of her golf cart to the cabin. She gave over the key to a

47

storage shed that was located behind the cabin that normally held water toys for the lake visitors during the summer months, but was empty now. "You can park your beautiful motorcycle in here to keep it safe from the frosty nights if you like. I always wanted Ralph to buy one, but he is afraid of them. If you're still here by the time we get back, can I have a ride? I haven't been on a bike before and I would really like to try it."

Future laughed, "Sure, Gladys, if I'm not here, and still in the area, I'll come by and we can cruise the town so all of your friends can see you wave at them if you'd like."

That sealed the deal for the older woman, and she was still smiling as she disappeared around the curved two track leading back to her place.

Chapter Five

"Are you fuckin' kidding me? Find her, and don't give me any shit about it either. Of all the bent dick bastards we have around here, you had to let her leave." The Prospect who had been at the gate last night was currently held a foot off the floor and being shaken like a rag in a high wind. He'd been the unfortunate one to let the bitch on that pussy pink and black hog leave the compound, and he was about to piss his pants. It was a relief when the ham sized fist connected with his jaw and he no longer felt fear. He was knocked out on the floor.

Big Dog pointed his finger at the men in the room. "You find her, and you bring her to me. You let me deal with her when she gets here, do you overmedicated fucks understand simple instructions? We need her, she was at the meet that night, and she saw everything that happened. Each one of us lost someone or something that night, and if you bastards have fucked up two hard damn years of searching for her, someone's gonna be tagged John Doe, along with those two motherfuckers on ice."

Ten men left the room, the last one grabbed the limp arm of the Prospect and dragged him out the door with the rest. Five of them were ten year Bastards and five were patch overs from the Chiefs. Charlie remained with Big Dog.

"Not tryin' to piss you off, big man, but what did you expect her to do? Did you tell her that you needed to keep those Breed alive until the meeting?

You told me that she went apeshit when she seen them, and one was hated more than the other one. Would it have been so bad to let her have at him? Taking away her dagger first, I mean. She could've relieved some of that hate and might've calmed her down for a few days until you decided to tell her why you wanted her here."

His morning had already deteriorated way beyond shit. Merlin dragged his fried ass to the club and brought his goofy old lady, Muffy, with him. They wanted to see Oracle, and when they couldn't find her, they sent for him. After two hours of searching and questioning people, his temper got the better of him and he finally got some answers when he started busting heads.

If they didn't find her before the meeting on Tuesday, several people were going to die. He wanted to let Future, Oracle, or whatever the fuck her name was, to fuck up that big son-of-a-bitch, but revenge would have to wait. He'd been waiting almost three years for his portion, she could damn well wait her turn.

Crazy Charlie had a point, it wouldn't have hurt to let her break her knuckles on their worthless hides until she got tired. The only reason he hadn't allowed it was that he hadn't thought of it. That pissed him off a bit, but not enough to worry about it. When she was brought back, he would make the offer to her. If she behaved herself, he might even tell the reason for her presence. One thing was sure, he'd heard enough about that pussy pink bike. The feel of her body against his when he'd held her back from gutting Jarl, had been a surprise. He liked the way she fit, tucked in his embrace. Her little ass snuggled against the zipper of his jeans felt good. The feeling of her tits lying over his arm felt good too. The sight of her face when he'd finally let her loose made him want to pull her back into his arms and comfort her, let her know she might have a chance to gain the revenge she wanted. But he couldn't tell her that, he couldn't be soft on her, at least not until after the meeting. Once that was out of the way, he was going to have her in his bed, and find out if she smelled like mint and honey all over her body, or just where his nose had inhaled the scent at her neck while he'd had her in his arms. His face was close enough to see the pointed nipples under her cut. He'd looked down, intending to tell her to be calm, and got a look at those tips under that tight red shirt. Oh yeah, once the business was taken care of, he planned to find out what color her nipples were.

Three days later, 8:00 a.m. ...

Future rolled into the gates of the compound and parked the bike. The kid at the gate had waved her through as if he'd been expecting her. She walked into the front doors and only saw a few people lounging around in the communal game room/room for every event it was needed for. She wanted to laugh when she saw Demon, with his head between a woman's thighs, where he must have passed out. Both of them were sleeping.

There were a few such couples in various states of undress cuddled together, sleeping the night's activities away. A woman with an impressive set of breasts was wandering around the room, picking up articles of clothing, and dropping them where she found them, until she picked up a very small tank top and pulled it over her head.

Future continued on her way into the dining room/bar, and smelled freshly brewed coffee. She went to the buffet and filled a mug, adding cream and a half teaspoon of sugar before walking back to the table she'd claimed a few days ago. After two days of rest and struggling with her own demons, she was ready for whatever came her way. That resolve included being taunted by the sight of her nightmares and the cruel club President, Big Dog. She would wait, and when the time came, she would find a way to gain her revenge. If things went bad around here, she at least had a bolt hole to hide in until the heat was off.

By the time her second cup of coffee was halfway gone, she was growing bored. More people trickled into the room, and although there were several that she recognized, it was just like growing up here. No one to talk to. No one wanted to be seen talking to the nutcase who knew their secrets. The few couples that stumbled in together went their separate ways from the door into the room.

Demon, minus his late night snack, came through the door, rubbing his face and running his hand through his hair. He set a course straight to the bar, where a member named Tiny was setting up brews for those that were in need.

He sucked the beer down and reached for another one. Before he could put it to his lips, he let out a loud belch and rubbed his flat stomach, telling the bartender, "Breakfast of Champs." He tilted the bottle at the man and brought it to his lips to take a few slower swallows. He must have felt her amused gaze, because he turned her way and stopped with the beer halfway to his lips. He reached in his pocket and fought with the phone that was stuck between the seam and the facing. Once it was in his hand, he began scrolling for the right number, and Future was doing all she could not to laugh out loud. He slopped beer on the floor before setting the bottle on the bar, then he must have found the person he was searching for since he pushed the screen and brought the black box to his ear. He reached over with his now free hand and grabbed his beer.

She didn't catch what he said, but she was pretty sure it was a call concerning her presence at the club, from the way he kept staring at her. She shook her head at his stare and got up to refill her coffee, and see if there was a stray Danish or biscuit that looked fairly fresh for her breakfast.

She found herself shoved back down on the chair and the coffee cup fell from her hand and shattered on the floor next to her. "You stay right the fuck put. No more disappearing, no more running around worrying everyone." The Demon he was named after was showing in his eyes. They were narrowed and cold. The term stone faced filtered through her mind.

She'd vowed to handle whatever came her way today or she would have given him a piece of her mind since his seemed to be still lying between that girl's thighs. "I was going to get a refill and grab something to eat. I've been here for over an hour already, so I think you can relax."

He yelled over his shoulder, "Pressley, get your ass over here." Although Demon never took his eyes off her to see the young Prospect run to his side, she saw it, and shook her head at him. "Tell him what you want and he'll get it."

She smiled at the young man with the small bull ring in the cartilage of his nose, "Coffee, cream, half teaspoon of sugar please, and if there is a Danish or something I would love one, thank you."

She waited until the kid left and asked him, "What's got your panties in a twist? From what I saw when I got here, you should have woke up in a good mood. Instead, you're acting like I'm going to steal something."

Demon wasn't speaking to her either it seemed. Pressley came back with her coffee, and a small plate with donut holes and half slices of French toast. She smiled at him again and told him thanks, before eating her sugary meal.

The coffee was gone, Demon was on his third beer, and he'd finally stopped looming over her, sitting himself in a chair near enough to grab her if she tried to run. He still hadn't spoken to her and they'd been sitting there for over an hour when she decided she'd had enough. She needed to see her parents and more pressing, she needed to pee.

She stood and began walking to the room she assumed was the bathroom. If he tried to stop her, there might be a puddle on the floor soon. He didn't try to stop her, he followed her into the room, and waited while she sat in the stall and did her thing. He waited until she'd washed her hands, and followed her from the small room. If he was going to go to her parents, they might draw the conclusion that she was involved with one of the members and it would tickle them to death. She ought to put him through such torture, but even for fun, there was no way she would take a man that smelled like some other woman's crotch across the street, let alone to her parents' home.

She tried one more time, "Demon, I know you are thinking I plan to run, why I have no idea. But if I promise to stay right here, will you please go wash the smell of old tuna fish off your face, it stinks, and while I normally wouldn't say a thing, you're the one insisting on sitting here. I'm the one being tortured."

Tiny heard every word and shouted in laughter. Demon shot him an evil look, but it was wasted, because Tiny was bent at the waist laughing so hard tears ran down his chubby cheeks. "She's right, man, I never say anything, 'cause I have the same problem when the old lady needs to be serviced. Damn, bro, she's got you pinned. Go ahead, I'll watch her until you get back." He chuckled, "I'll have Pressley chase her down and I'll sit on her, she won't get far." He began laughing again and several men who were still in the room, laughed because

Tiny was laughing. They had no idea why he was laughing, but his high pitch was hilarious.

Demon gave her a warning look, and nodded to his replacement. "I'll be ten minutes tops."

Future asked Tiny if he had a broom and dust pan, and was handed one to clean up the broken cup. She handed the things back, and he handed her a wet cloth to mop up the sticky mess that had dried while Demon insisted on her ass being glued to the chair. She moved herself to the bar, because Tiny seemed like the friendly type and they exchanged quips and bar jokes. She offered to send him a book with several bar games in it, from beer pong to balancing bottles on foreheads doing a walking obstacle course. "We have game night at the Petite Bruja, every other Friday. It's our busiest night and you'll be surprised at how many people participate."

Demon was back within his self allotted time, but he wasn't wearing a shirt, so she teased him about trolling for the chickie babies. "Damn, boy, don't you get enough women chasing after you without having to advertise those nipple studs?"

The arrival of Big Dog saved him from answering her playful comments. If he'd fucked her like he wanted to back when he met her, maybe the thought of busting her wouldn't bother him so much. He didn't want to like her, especially after the past couple of days while she was missing, and the Prez raged around the place, busting heads and demanding results. Once he found out that she'd come back on her own, he could just about guess what Big Dog was going to say about the men's abilities to find their asses with both hands. He would be right too. The urgency to bring her back was doubled last night when a call came through from Lucifer's Breed. They wanted the meeting to take place tonight, they didn't want to wait until Tuesday.

The only reason they could have for the accelerated timeline was that someone must have been discussing club business outside of the compound. Somehow, they'd found out the star witness was found, and now was missing, and wanted to push the talks up as fast as they could. Demon knew Big Dog was concerned she might have been taken. Dorsey was still on the loose and her very presence made a lie out of his story of attempted heroism that night.

Big Dog knew she was there, but he was almost too mad to speak. He'd seen the pussy bike and as far as a woman's ride, it was fine, black with orange flames would be more his style. He walked up to her and held out his hand. "Keys." He wasn't asking, he was demanding. When she stubbornly shook her head no, he didn't ask again. "Demon, get Chewy to help you put that pussy bike in the warehouse, and take the front tire off, before you leave it."

She was furious, and let him know in no uncertain terms, "What the hell? You can't do that. I came here under my own steam, no one had to drag me here. I haven't broken any rules, and this is bullshit. The club's rules state that I can leave in good standing anytime I wish." She folded her arms and gave him a narrow-eyed look that she used in the bar at home. Of course at the Petite Bruja, that look usually meant she was reaching for the baseball bat behind the bar.

He stood looming over her and grinned, "You just refused an order from the club's president. I do believe that is a rule broken, a big one." He had her, she would have to agree to whatever he wanted now, if she wanted her ride back. After talking to Charlie, he knew he would need to have something she wanted to gain her cooperation. Since letting her seriously hurt or possibly kill the leverage, he had to bring Lucifer's Breed President back to the field, wasn't going to happen, yet.

With her testimony in front of both clubs, revenge would be his and the Chiefs, who were now patched over to the Burning Bastards MC.

His plan to challenge a territory line had been met with resistance, and he no longer gave a shit what Lucifer's Breed demanded. He was up to his ass in hints and innuendos about the Breed's plans to "School the Bastards, like they'd schooled the Chiefs."

Tonight, any schooling would be done by him.

He needed to keep her busy for a few hours before it would be time to leave for this meeting. "Georgie, get Merlin and his old lady, they've been worried about their long lost Oracle. I know they would like to see her in the flesh before she does her disappearing act again. Bring them to the lounge, and tell him to leave the herb at home. The last thing any of us needs is to get a contact buzz from that shit tonight."

The rat bastard grabbed her arm and pulled her out of the room, down that hall, and this time took the stairs up. The landing was a big room with several comfortable spots to crash, or play video games. He shoved her into the thick cushions of an easy chair and sat on the ottoman in front of her.

"This is the thing, we have a meeting with Lucifer's Breed tonight." He let that sink in and was gratified to see her eyes widen a little and her nose began to flare. Maybe old Crazy Charlie was right. If he told her what's going on, it might gain her cooperation. "I can't let any lasting harm come to the prisoners until tonight, and there is a big chance their own people will take care of your need for revenge. Lucifer's Breed upper management doesn't have a clue what some of their enforcers are doing, and it appears that when they find out after the fact, they are reluctant to take care of it. Their club has gotten so big that it's hard to keep track.

"I don't give free passes, those motherfucker's know me, they waited until I had to fly out to bury my parents, and they fucking attacked like the rats they are, in the middle of the night. It took me two long damned years to track down the story, and who did what. Charlie told you, we all thought you were dead, until Butch's old lady told him about treating a girl with extensive injuries that was found on a dirt road naked and half dead. She described the tat on your back, and the one on the back of your neck. Poppa, Tiny, and Lorenzo, the guy that did the artwork, all agreed that it had to be you.

"This all came to light almost a year after that fucking softtail disappeared from the lot here. Everyone called you the little witch, hell, I never even knew your real name until I got your father in here to tell me what this Oracle we were looking for was. We found the bar, when Tarzan and Needles got out of jail, and stopped in the place for a beer. They came back and told Tiny about the name of the place and he looked it up. O M Smith is the taxpayer, and all we could get out of Merlin was him saying we should find the Oracle. He kept saying shit like, "The Oracle will tell you what happened, find the Oracle."

They could hear the clatter of feet on the stairs and Big Dog stood and headed for the stairs. "We leave at seven, be ready." Her parents came into view and she could see the years hadn't been friendly to the aging hippies.

They'd been in their early thirties when she was born. That might have contributed to the reason they considered her a gift from God and the bearer of good news. She'd missed them, as silly and marshmallow brained as her mother was, the woman had never forgotten to remind her daughter that she was loved. Merlin had always been her biggest fan, and would brag to anyone listening about his Oracle and her special gifts. He loved her too, maybe he went a bit far with bragging, but she always knew he was there for her. It had hurt when she thought they'd left her for dead.

She suffered through the embrace of each of them and felt the bones protruding, and the fragility of their bodies. Her mother retained her beauty in the sparkle of her eyes, but the climb up the steps left the woman shaking and Future helped her sit into the soft cushions of the sofa. Merlin wore a crafty look in his eyes and she knew he was going to start with his interrogation. She answered them, but skirted the more painful memories and spent the time talking about her bar and home. She promised to visit them at home before she left. She helped her mother to escape the sofa's soft cushions. Since it was dinnertime, they all went down to the dining room and Muffy sat at a table to keep a spot for them, while Future and her father filled her a plate and got her a cup of tea.

She left them still eating their dinner, and made her way to the front door where several men were already gearing up. Her bike was nowhere to be seen and she was becoming agitated. She looked around and saw a shiny Dodge backed up close to the side door of the club, and four men were wrestling two long wooden boxes into the bed. It didn't take more than a moment's speculation for her to conclude the boxes contained guns, not handguns. From the number of bikes and riders present, it appeared this party wasn't only serious, it would be epic.

Five old ladies were tagging along, and several greybeards were milling around, waiting to be assigned a task. The women and older members were driving the two trucks. One was towing an enclosed trailer, and it was obvious the truck's bed was loaded down too, but fiberglass lids were lowered to keep others from seeing what was being transported.

Big Dog came out, flanked by his handpicked men. It was obvious he planned to make a show of strength, and when he called her over, and told her that she was riding with him, she balked. "I want my bike."

Chapter Six

He didn't have time for this shit, she would be safe with him and the vanguard. What the fuck was her problem? "Give me one good reason that you're acting all prissy right now, 'cause I have to tell you, I'm not impressed. You can ride in the box on the way back, but you will get your ass on my bike, and you will shut the fuck up now."

She was shaking her head no and the only way to make him understand why she wanted her bike, would tell him one of the lessons she'd learned that night, the night that her world changed forever. "I ride my transportation, I can't trust that you will be there when I need to leave, I don't trust anyone, so don't think you're special. I was left at the mercy of those animals once before, shoved to the jackals so Dorsey could get away. If I'd been allowed to ride my own bike that night, I would have been gone before they could keep me."

He could hear the fear, see it, and he understood her reason for being stubborn. "You see these men?" He jerked his thumb over his shoulder, "touch them, touch each one of them on the way to my bike, if one of them would leave you to be harmed in anyway, he stays here. No questions asked. One way or the other, your happy ass will be on that bike with me." He dragged her to the first man, and ordered him to hold out his hand. Out of the ten men she'd touched, only one was iffy in her mind, but that might have been because he was shitfaced and held his liquor well enough to ride. He almost looked relieved when Big Dog called Needles over to take his place.

She had to take a few deep breaths before she hoisted herself on the big machine, but once she was seated, he shook his head, and pointed to the Tryke next to the hog. "Not tonight, witch woman, you get to ride bitch in style. This is a show, and we always deliver." She climbed on and was happy that she wouldn't need to hold his middle while she sat on a four by six inch pad of leather behind him. This seat was much better, and from the looks given him by a few of his men, she felt warmed when she realized that he'd decided to take the three wheeler at the last minute. She was still nervous, but his offer and the way he kept his word about replacing any man she didn't trust, went a long way to calming her enough to keep her on the seat.

The drive seemed to take forever, and her guts were twisting from anxiety, but she felt no fear about this meeting. The place was what bothered her. When they pulled onto the dirt two track, she began scanning the woods around them. It had been so long since she'd deliberately tried to use her gift of sight, she worried she might miss something important. When the energies of Lucifer's Breed came within her range of second sight, she leaned down and cupped her hand to his ear to tell him, "There's at least fifty people ahead, and I think there's a lot more further down, I can feel them."

He didn't say anything, his head nodded and he increased the speed of the Tryke a little. She knew he was showing his disdain for needing a shield or escort. They would be the first sight Lucifer's Breed would see coming. It was both brave and stupid of him, but she felt the power he was ready to display building in his aura. She kept her hands on his leather-clad shoulders, and hung on over the bumpy terrain.

The sight that met her eyes reminded her of the old westerns on TV. When the cowboys looked up and saw a wide line of Indians watching them from above. Only the sea of bikes wasn't above them, and no rocks to hide behind, except for the one she already sat behind. She leaned forward again and told him, "That is about half of them, the rest are on the other side of those trees."

Big Dog figured as much when they'd started out to get here. Lucifer's Breed were not stupid, at least not the National boys, they would never trust a rival club as large as the Burning Bastards. For the same reason, only ten of his men would be at the initial meet and greet, but thirty would be in the background, and another fifty were staying hidden in the wooded two track. One of the pick-ups would be directly behind the ten men behind his back. He wasn't about to show them anything but confidence and strength. He stopped the Tryke ten feet from the line and saw his men pulling up beside him, flanking his sides, and two parked behind his rear wheels.

The large tent that was a military Field Officer's style, sat squarely in the center. They could plainly see two men flanking a bearded older man heading for the tent. Seven others lined up behind the shelter, all of which would scare anyone in their right mind.

"Stay on the Tryke. Don't get off unless I call you, I mean it. I won't want to bust you one in front of these people, but I will. You need to believe that, I will do it. Everything you say after the fact will be held suspect, so do us both a favor, just do as I've told you."

She believed him. He wouldn't hit a woman in anger unless he had no choice, at least not that she could feel. He was also giving her protection if something bad happened. Four of the men, including the club's VP, Butch, stayed with the bikes and her, the rest followed a few paces behind him as they walked out to meet Lucifer's Breed's President, and his men.

Big Dog moved forward and his men went with him. It surprised her to see Demon and Knight stayed outside, while Freakshow and Seth went in with their Prez. The waiting began. There were no friendly words exchanged between the two clubs' members, only intimidating stares. An hour went by, then another, the men waiting to fight if needed took turns sitting on the grass and standing. One of the club's scantily clad bitches took a case of brew out to the Bastards, she got swats on the ass and offers to allow her to take care of their other thirsts.

Freakshow came out of the meeting and walked back to where Butch was waiting, after few minutes of discussion, the VP nodded his head and the two men came over to her.

"Get down, and try not to act like a martyr. You are a witness, and it's show and tell time. All you have to do is tell your story, don't argue, don't elaborate, and for God's sake don't show disrespect to anyone in the room. This is your chance for the revenge that Big Dog says you want, don't fuck it up."

Freak led her into the tent, and she could feel the tension the Bastards were hiding so well. The bearded man must be the President of Lucifer's Breed, and the others his lieutenants. Those were his most trusted allies along with his bodyguards. Just the same as any club, the President surrounded himself, many times they were VPs, Sgts at Arms, and Suits, or Lawyers.

Big Dog nodded at her, looked at his counterpart, and introduced her as Oracle.

"She was there the night of the meeting, she saw everything." He turned his attention back on her and said, "Talk, tell us everything that happened that night and afterwards."

The bearded President piped up, "Hang on a minute, if you're going to waste my time bringing your fuck doll here to shovel shit in my lap, forget it."

Big Dog shook his head, "I haven't tapped that yet. I might at some point, but I have more important things to think about than trying to fuck this up by screwing a witness. One that took almost three years to track down. There's no history here." He nodded at Future.

Future talked, she looked at the bearded leader and kept her eyes on his. "Everyone was drinking, and those who had partners available, were having sex. Frenchy was playing his guitar by one of the campfires, everything was peaceful. The bikes ran over bedrolls, scattered stuff, and the men shot tasers at random people. One of your men carried a sawed-off shotgun and I heard it go off, but didn't see who got hit. I was almost to the bikes when Dorsey grabbed me and shoved me behind him to get the two Breed off his ass that were chasing him.

"Reeker and several others forced themselves on me, when I fought back, he punched me out. The next thing I knew, I was tied to a hook in a cabin by a wide leather collar and a leash. They made me watch as they beat Frenchy to death, and Reeker hung Frenchy's body upside down by his feet. They made me watch as they kicked his head into hamburger." She was doing her best not to vomit from the remembered smell of blood and the sight of Frenchy when they'd finally finished with him.

"Jarl, Reeker, Mule and another man that I never heard his name, they held me there for over three weeks, torturing and violating my body. The last night I think they planned to kill me, but wanted to have their fun first." She went on with her story and told them about waking up in the hospital. She stood with her hands at her sides, waiting to be dismissed.

Bearded man smiled at her. "Now let me get this straight, Jarl and Mule claimed to be the club President and Vice?" At her nod, he continued, "So, you had sex for a few weeks with my boys, and had to tell your old man the reason you played rabbit and ran that night. Rather than tell him the truth, you make up a story about abuse and being tortured for sympathy. So now you have to keep the story, right?"

The six men in the room were staring at her. All she had to prove her words were the scars she carried. She didn't want to do what had to be done, thinking of the revulsion she knew she would see once they saw her scars was enough to make her want to run, but the only way to gain what she wanted was to do it.

She began with her boots, and shimmied out of her tight jeans. Her colors were handed to Freakshow and she stared at the skeptical leader of Lucifer's Breed, as she pulled her t-shirt over her head, reached behind her back and unhooked her bra, then straightened up and dared him to say she had enjoyed one minute of the torture his men had done to her. She stepped back two steps to let them see the whole front and turned around slowly to stare at the canvas wall behind her. She let them look their fill, and raised her hands to pull her long hair to the front of her body, so the men could see the carved words in her skin, half of which were melted together in a grotesque mess of shiny purple and red skin. She heard "Holy fuck, did he actually carve wings in her shoulders? FALLEN and an A and an N." There were other words, but when she heard someone gagging, she hung her head. She had to turn and face them again, had to tell them there was more, and she knew she was crying, but silent tears were all she had to help her relieve the hurt their words and the humiliation their lack of trust in her word carried.

"There is more if you need to see them. The nails they used to pierce my, my, they used nails. The police have them. I no longer have a spleen, and I had lost so much blood, the doctors were ready to pronounce me when I got to the hospital. You can get the records with all of your contacts I am sure."

Big Dog was mad, she looked at him when he stood and stomped over to her, jerking her t-shirt from Freakshow and placing it in her hands. "Get dressed, if they need to see more they can fuck themselves." He told Seth to take her back to the bike and get her a drink.

The leader of Lucifer's Breed said "No, let her stay," and said something low to his men. One left, and she got dressed the rest of the way, stuffing her bra into the waistband of her pants, because she wasn't about to take the shirt off again. She didn't know where to look, or what she was supposed to do, so she stood where she was, and waited. The small leather case that contained her ID and credit card had fallen to the ground and she looked up to thank Freakshow for finding it. She was gratified to see he wasn't repulsed by her. He gave her a small smile, and nodded. That had to have hurt the normally frozen faced "Goth Daddy" as she thought of when she thought of him.

Big Dog spoke and she watched Lucifer's Breed's people as he addressed their leader. "We didn't come here to have a war, but we will be happy to oblige if you are still skeptical about our reasons for keeping your boys on ice until this meeting. The question is, what are you going to do about it?" He sent Seth to get the truck.

They heard the powerful motor of the three quarter ton Ram as it backed up to the line where the Bastards' bikes were parked.

Fires had been built due to the darkness, and the two lieutenants were told to go bring in the crates, Big Dog called their leader by name. "Wolfman, this is my gift to Lucifer's Breed, what you do with it determines how these negotiations end."

The crates were too big to be opened in the tent, so they hauled them back outside. They were set close to one of the open campfires, and two of the Breed opened the lids with pry bars. Jarl was in the first crate, naked, with his hands and ankles duct taped together. The wide tape was plastered over his mouth, and the leader reached down and yanked it off.

There were a few small bruises on his face, but the rest of him wasn't marred in any recent way. The burn scar on his lower cheek and jaw was coffee colored, but that wasn't new. Two of Wolfman's crew stood him upright in the box, but no one moved to cut the bindings holding him in place.

They opened the second crate and found Reeker in similar shape. Mule was brought to the campfire by two burly men, and until he saw Future standing on the opposite side of the fire, he hadn't resisted his captivity. The back of his head carried scars from the fire, his hair was gone, and the scars had been tattooed over.

She'd thought the men died in the fire, but obviously, the fourth man must have saved them, and dumped her in that field. Her fists clenched and

71

released. She wanted to hurt them, she wanted to break every bone in Jarl's body, cut his dick off and listen to him scream and beg for mercy.

The man called Wolfman approached Jarl and backhanded him. "You told me the Chiefs and the Bastards attacked our men. You told me they came into *our* territory and attacked *our* people, stole the money that belonged to the club." Each time Wolfman knocked the big man down, two Breed pulled him to his feet. "You have never been a President, an enforcer, or a goddamned anything but trouble. You disgraced our club, you kill people for fun, and we all know I have no problem with killing an enemy, everyone knows that.

"When you use an enemy's woman, I consider that spoils of war. You don't fuck up a helpless woman like you did. What kind of man has to keep a woman chained like a fucking dog? You use them and lose them, you don't torture them for fun. Not like that. I could maybe deal if she was an evil bitch that caused personal problems for you, this shit ain't nothin' but psycho shit, and we got enough psychos."

Where the Prez of Lucifer's Breed pulled his dagger from Future didn't see, she did see the blade shoved between Jarl's ribs. She saw the blade when Wolfman handed the hilt to her and told her to, "Carve the coward up, but don't kill him yet." She saw the evil bastard's eyes fill with fear when she fulfilled her fondest wish, the dagger was nice and sharp, and Jarl screamed before she handed the weapon back to its owner.

She didn't hear the groans from the crowds of men. She felt something deep inside let loose, and her spirit lighten. She surprised the man by politely thanking him. "You have no idea, no idea, of the nightmares I've suffered. Thank you." She walked back to stand between Demon and Charlie. The temptation to use that dagger to its fullest potential on both Jarl and Mule was strong, but she knew she wouldn't have been able to finish the job without pissing off the embarrassed Breed President. His concession to her would have to be good enough.

Mule was dealt with in a similar fashion, but no repeat offer came from the Breeds. They got the name Fred as the fourth man in the cabin that night. Fortunately for Fred, he'd died last year on a run, when his tires hit some gravel that had been shoved onto the pavement by a road truck or something. The lids on the wooden crates were nailed down. Reeker was another story.

His crate was given to Mule, but they had no intention of giving him the dirt nap. His cut and clothing was taken from the crate before the lid was nailed down, and he was cut loose from the duct tape bindings. "I'm not doing this because of the split tail, that was spoils of war, I'm not doing this because of the death of the Bastards man either. This is for lying to the club, to me, and pretending to be something you're not. Makes me think you might have designs on my back. You are done, your name will be stricken from any records as a member. You're gonna be shunned, any member seen with you, or that wishes to back you, will suffer the same fate. We are men, not fucking cowards like your friends there."

Wolfman handed Reeker's cut to his lieutenant, and the man tossed it into the closest fire. They turned their backs to the lone man who was dressing, and appearing to be holding back tears. Whether tears of relief at not suffering the fate his friends did, or for the loss of a club that was his family for over half of his lifetime, no one cared to question him. He began walking from the field and no one paid attention to him again, his bike would be outside the gates of the club when he got there.

The Presidents and their lieutenants went back to the tent. By six o'clock in the morning, they were all headed back to their clubs. There would be another meeting to solidify the truce, and an infancy of an alliance, but for now, everyone was satisfied with the outcome of the meeting.

Future didn't argue or get into one of the trucks on the way back, she climbed onto the bitch perch of the Tryke and let the cool autumn wind blow away any lingering doubts in her mind that her nightmare had been put to rest. She didn't delude herself into believing the bad dreams would end, but she knew they would not be as intense, and hopefully they would lesson over time.

Chapter Seven

All the way back to the club, Big Dog thought about the woman at his back. Seeing the scars she carried only bothered him when he thought of the suffering she had gone through, and lived to show and tell. Even that bastard, Wolfman, saw through her 'fuck you' attitude and felt some compassion. His words and actions, letting her use his personal blade to maim the motherfucking scum, Jarl, showed the man carried a small bit of humanity in his soul somewhere.

He knew confronting Wolfman with a witness was the only way to open the communication between the clubs. Now the counties between the clubs would be considered neutral territory. He'd been as shocked as everyone else in the tent to see Future strip down to her panties to prove her words. Her body must have been perfection before the imprisonment.

He'd been attracted to her before now, but he wanted to give her time to get used to him. Women either backed off after seeing his prick, or they viewed it as a challenge. He knew that if he tried to romance her now, she would think he was either a freak that got off on her scars, or he felt sorry for her. The truth was he wanted her—period. Demon and Knight both told him she had something about her that made a man want to lay down with her and fuck until neither of them could move. He'd laughed at the time, walking away from offered pussy was never a problem for him. If he was in the

mood to have sex, all he had to do was snap his
fingers in the club. There was always a house cat or
a bitch as some called them at the club, or even a
fluffer looking for a little action. Though a house
cat was looking to eventually settle down with a
brother.

Since the incident with her disappearing act,
Demon told him that he had decided he wanted
someone more docile and submissive. He was a
dominant, and had no plans to change his ways,
even for a woman like Future.

Knight hadn't changed his mind about her, he
confessed to having a lingering passion for her. "It's
fucked up, man, I don't want to lock down with her,
I just want to fuck her. Don't get me wrong, she's
nice enough, and I like her, but she is too
independent for me to have as an old lady. I need a
woman that needs me; that one doesn't need
anything from anybody."

Big Dog wasn't sure he liked the idea of being
led into a full out relationship, but he was planning
a private thank you party for her before she drove
away on her pussy bike.

They got to the club and everyone went their
separate ways. Future was eyeing the sofas in the
lounge, but found herself pulled out of the back
door and led to one of the duplexes behind the main
building. Big Dog pushed her through the doorway
and followed her inside. The place was sparsely
furnished with two recliners and a small love seat.
A 55-inch flat screen took up one entire wall, and
there was a long skinny table between the spots to
sit. A small kitchen that sported a toaster, a stack of

paper plates, and a Bunn coffeemaker on the short counter, was best described as functional.

She headed for the two closed doors and was thankful to find the bathroom on the first try. Seeing the shower and a stack of folded towels, she didn't resist the temptation. She reached over, locked the bathroom door, and stripped before she could change her mind. She felt dirty after her show and tell, and all she had thought about was a hot shower to wash the feelings of humiliation away. The heated water would also help relax the muscles in her back, hopefully enough for her to be able to sleep for a few hours before she hit the road home.

By the time she was dressed and ready to leave the room, she was wide awake. It would take a couple more hours before she would be in dreamland, although she hated the thought of staying another night, it was something to consider. She still had to ask Big Dog if she had paid a high enough penalty for him to release her bike.

She smelled fresh brewed coffee, headed for the pot, and the mug next to it was filled within seconds. A box of sugar packets sat on the counter and next to them was creamer packets. Tearing open two of the sugar packets made her think of Crazy Charlie, and the prank she'd played on Demon and Knight. She had a small 'ha ha' moment when she remembered the greed in the waitress's eyes, and wondered if she would ever find out if Charlie had gotten a little 'extra' special somethin' that night.

Big Dog was still in the living room area watching the morning news shows when she walked over to sit and drink her coffee. He shut the TV off and sat back, drinking from his own mug, and asked how she felt.

"I hope you don't mind, I took a shower. I needed to feel clean. I do feel much better now though."

He leaned forward with his elbows on his knees, cradling the warm mug in his hands. "How long do you plan to stay?"

The question brought her out of her thoughts about him. "I guess I'll get a few hours of sleep today and hit the road before it gets too late. If I oversleep, I'll leave tomorrow morning, as long as a certain bossy club President gives my bike back and I have his blessing to leave." She gave him a small smile. "I wouldn't want to break any more rules after all." He nodded and sat back in the deep cushioned chair and she asked, "Can I ask you a personal question?"

"Depends on what it is that you want to ask. No, I haven't killed anyone lately, I am six feet seven and a half inches tall, I don't know what I weigh. No, I didn't play basketball, and the weather reports I leave to the slick bald headed guy that tells me if it's gonna rain on the six o'clock news." He laid his head back a bit more looking at the ceiling, and continued his list of most asked questions.

"I am a Leo, I don't eat little children, steal purses from old ladies, or stomp hobbits. Yes, I have a name, it's Hugh Dougherty, so the tag Big Dog has been with me since high school. I am thirty-five years old and have most of my own teeth. Oh yeah, I wear a size eighteen shoe, and contrary to popular opinion, I was born not hatched or found under a rock." He grinned her way. "And yes, it's true what they say about a man's feet and hands being big. Not bragging, just answering the questions that I normally get asked."

"I have a few questions of my own. Like why did you disappear like that, instead of going to the Prez, or one of the others? And more importantly, for the here and now, I want to know what you think about being fucked by a man like me. If you have issues with sex after the way those assholes fucked you up, I can deal. Tell the truth, I have to admire your courage. I know grown men who have been fucked up with fire and more, that couldn't stand in front of a bunch of men and show their scars. You got guts and dignity, and I like that in a woman. I was attracted before your striptease, so don't think too damn hard on the subject. I had to wait, and my cock isn't used to waiting when it feels an interest, if you feel me." He grimaced and shifted in his seat.

Could he have just offered to, "Wait, are you saying you want to have sex with me, even after seeing my body? I tried it once since that night. You asked if I was fucked up because of it? The answer is hard to explain, I'm not sure I can explain it. I have a few issues, but I can function if that's what you want to know. The one guy, he was a freak about the scars, he liked them, but I picked up needs during after that time with those men while on the leash. I'm not exactly proud of those needs now, so I don't talk about them, even to make you understand why getting involved with me isn't a

79

good idea for any sane man." She stood to take the mug into the kitchen, she was so damn tired that she could fall asleep in the chair with him. He would be surprised if she grabbed him to cuddle against like the overstuffed pillow that was on her bed for those times her emotions got out of hand before she slept.

He saw that she was finished with her coffee, and took the mug from her fingers, and placed both mugs on the table. He stood and she felt tiny standing beside him. His hands went to her waist and he bent over her, zeroing his lips onto hers. His tongue demanded entrance, and since she resisted, his teeth bit down on her bottom lip making her moan and open her mouth under his. His tongue slid over hers, topping it and sweeping throughout her mouth, exploring every nook and cranny, retreating and pushing inside time after time, until she had to break the seal he'd set in order to breathe. Her t-shirt was pulled over her head as she tried to hold onto the cotton material, but he bound her hands in one of his, and used the shirt to tangle her wrists together over her head. She brought them down and tried to untangle them, but he nibbled her neck and told her, "Be still, you're going to like this."

He licked down her collarbone and down her chest until he came to the stainless steel barbells she had in her pierced nipples. His groan and the way his tongue and teeth tormented one and in turn, the other, had her catching her breath. He grew restless and licked and kissed his way to the waistband of her jeans, and growled a frustrated sound.

Instead of stripping the jeans off there in his living room, he picked her up, laying his mouth over hers, and started walking to the room she hadn't opened the door to as of yet. She was tossed backwards on the big bed and his hands were at the waistband of her jeans again. This time he unsnapped and unzipped the denim and peeled it down her legs. She wasn't wearing panties, and he rested his head on her belly. "I love this, you're so fuckin' hot. I want inside you so bad I might shoot my load before I get near this pretty pink pussy of yours."

He sat back on his heels and spread her thighs to see what he'd missed earlier when she stood in front of the six men in the tent. Her labia had hole marks, and the vulva had several indents that looked like someone had cut them with scissors. It was a sexy sight, but he wouldn't have made a woman go through something that painful. Even the hood over her clit had been slit wide open. "I'll be damned, I know this had to have been painful when it was done, but I swear it looks just like a fuckin' butterfly on a rose."

She was trying to close her legs and he wasn't about to let her. "It's ugly and my scars are ugly and you are just being nice, or you're horny or something; maybe you get off on deformed people. This isn't going to work, I need to leave." She was too embarrassed to listen to his lies. For whatever reason he wasn't yet repulsed, but she knew better than to let it go any farther. She began to double her efforts to leave his bed, sitting up, only to be pushed back down by one of his wide spread hands. She tried to roll her hips and let out a small squeal when he slapped her between her open legs. It wasn't exactly painful, but it certainly stung.

"Look at me, woman," he tapped her again, and she took a deep breath, opened her eyes and closed them and opened them again to look at his face. She hated crying at the best of times, but she was looking at him through a thick layer of tears pooling in the corner of her eyes, and sat up, swinging a fist at him when he pulled his phone from his back pocket and punched two buttons. She thought he was going to be cruel enough to take a picture of her deformed body. Instead, he had actually called someone to come to his place to see something, "Yeah, I want your opinion on something I have here. The door is open."

Within minutes they could hear the door opening and closing. She closed her eyes and his command to open them was ignored. Another swat got him a glare of defiance and when she saw Knight walk into the room, it pissed her off more. "You are a mean son-of-a-bitch and I…" The look on Knight's face stopped her words. Big Dog had moved from his spot between her legs and she hadn't realized it until Knight had replaced him. His hands and fingers opened her thighs as wide as possible, and he kept staring.

"Would you look at this beauty, baby, I know this had to hurt, but dayum, look at you. The colors and the way this beauty opens, it looks like a butterfly sippin' on a flower." She watched as he licked his lips and bent closer. "Sorry, Big Dog, but I gotta have a taste of this, you can't put her in front of me like you did and expect me to walk away, my dick is as hard as a fucking log." He clamped his mouth down on her and within a few minutes, she forgot her humiliation, she forgot she was mad at the men, she forgot her own name as pleasure washed over her.

He climbed from between her legs and off the bed to shed his shirt and groaned as Big Dog laid his naked body down next to her and pulled her over the top, positioning her where his prick waited to fill her depths. He concentrated on his breathing and control as his hands pushed her hips down, splitting her folds and widening her channel with every inch of his cock.

He was right, his joke about his feet and hands wasn't so much of a joke. His thickness was widening her to the point she didn't think she could stretch any further, but his hands continued to push her hips down and his prick up. He drew back and slammed up to penetrate the last few inches of her depths and she screamed as his cock slammed into her cervix. She came apart, shattering into a million pieces and digging her nails into his shoulders to keep from falling.

"Now, I want you to ride me, hard and deep. You're so fucking tight I'm not gonna last long if I do the work. Take what you need. Knight is waiting his turn, but only if you want him to join in." She clamped down over his cock when he mentioned Knight's eager willingness to join them. He looked over at his enforcer and nodded his head, signaling his permission to take her unsuspecting asshole, while he enjoyed her snatch.

"Knight is going to fuck your ass while you fuck my cock, is that okay with you, baby?" He pulled on the heavy bars in her nipples and gave them a short twist to gain her attention. "I asked if Knight can fuck you in the ass, yes or no."

She couldn't believe he had to ask, there were two fingers buried in her back hole already and the burning stretching heightened her pleasure. "Yes, yes, just, yes." Almost immediately, she felt the thick head of Knight's prick replacing his fingers. The stinging burn became a stretching pain and she screamed, clenching both her vaginal muscles and sphincter over their cocks, making both men moan loudly.

"Holy fuck. Damn, woman, let up so I can get in the rest of the way. Dog, you need to pull out so I can go deep a few times." He would be lucky to get a few strokes inside her tight ass, but damn if he wasn't going to try to make sure she came when he did. Big Dog pulled out until his cock was just inside the ring of muscle guarding her entrance, and he continued his journey into her tight ass. The way she sat back onto his cock blew his mind. She wanted deeper, she was gonna get deeper. His hands went to her ass cheeks and he pulled them apart as wide as possible to penetrate another inch, while she continued to try to move on both pricks.

His mouth kissed and licked his way over her scars with no hesitation, and when he bit down on the tender skin just below her ear, she began moving faster, almost slamming herself onto his and Big Dog's cocks. The wailing scream signaled her release.

84

When he felt her release, Big Dog let loose his jizz at the mouth of her womb. He couldn't believe how much he came, but then he hadn't been so thoroughly wrung out like this in years, and all he could do now was to let her body milk the last drops of come from over his sensitized prick.

When both men slid deep that last time, she was done, the orgasm that took her over was so intense it made her scream out loud and her body continued to twitch long after the contractions of her inner muscles eased up enough for their pricks to leave her holes. She was still sandwiched between their big bodies, and it felt like the safest place in the world to her. Knight was massaging the cheeks of her ass and thighs, and began to rub her back with firm long stokes. It was new to her, this tender after sex treatment. Big Dog was slowly licking his way over and down her collarbone while massaging her head and ears. Who would have thought that having your head rubbed would feel so good? The last thing she thought of before she drifted to sleep was that she shouldn't get used to this kind of treatment.

Knight left her with a last kiss on the ravaged wing of the broken angel on her shoulder blade. He and the big guy exchanged nods, and he gathered his clothes and left.

Chapter Eight

Future woke to the feel of lips caressing her neck and the top of her shoulders. She was on her back, and Big Dog was lying between her thighs, while his prick rested its head just inside the entrance to her vaginal tunnel. His lips found the path to her nipples and he licked and sucked them into hard points and his tongue and teeth scraped and teased the hard nubs until he was satisfied then he glanced up to look into her sleepy eyes.

"Hello, beautiful. If you have an objection to a bit of afternoon screwing, save it. It's too late to stop now, baby." He pushed forward with his hips and sent his big cock sliding through her tunnel, over the slightly sore muscles left over from this morning's round of sex. His cock kissed the mouth of her cervix, and retreated, only to nudge the small funnel on every third or fourth down stroke.

She wrapped her legs around his pistoning hips and pulled herself up, to enjoy his thrusts at a different angle and making his strokes penetrate deeper without impediment.

"Oh yeah, that's good," she told him how much she loved his fat prick. "I want you, and I'm glad the feeling is mutual. I feel so full when you're deep inside of me." His finger began to torment her exposed clit, and it felt like an electric shock. She was no longer talking, her gasps and groans heard escaping through her gritted teeth let him know she was thoroughly enjoying his efforts to pleasure them both. She yanked on her nipples and squeezed her breasts. He bent his head and bit her nipple. She felt the muscles of his ass cheeks beneath her hand and reached to grab both of them, pulling him into her depths as hard as she could pull. She wanted hard and punishing, but he pulled back. "What the hell? Why did you stop?"

He rolled her over onto all fours and she rested her head on her forearms. Her, "Ah, okay, this will work," was cut short by a cry, as she felt him smacking her ass with his open palm. His thrust in sent him deep, and with the outstroke she got a smack on the ass. There was something so exciting about his dominating actions that she shivered in anticipation of each smack. His thrusts became urgent, and his fingers of his left hand gripped her hip, his right hand wound her hair around his fist and he pulled her head back to lean over and kiss her lips as she cried out, and bit at his lips. She couldn't hold back any longer and reached for the colors bursting in her brain with each contraction of her muscles gripping his prick. He shouted as she felt his liquid shooting into her body. The heated sperm felt fantastic running over her sensitized inner flesh. "Oh yes, all of it."

*****

She napped while he showered and by the time she woke, it was dinnertime. Her saddlebags were hanging on the foot of the bed, so she grabbed her clean t-shirt and jeans, and headed for a hot shower herself. She felt wonderful. She hadn't thought about her scarred body at all today, until she saw Knight standing by the bar, talking to Tiny and Big Dog. Her blush was wasted on the men. Knight walked over to her and raised his hand to her cheek, cradling it in his wide palm. "I didn't get the chance to say thank you. So please accept my humble thank you for fulfilling my wish since I first saw you fucking that stripper pole at the Bruja." He gave her a smile and wandered off in the direction of the lounge.

She shook her head. It was a habit to clear the scenes she'd just felt, Knight should be warned, but why should she warn him about his impending future. If he knew what was happening, he would run far and fast. *No need to scare him*, at least not right now. She lined up at the buffet and loaded her plate with fruit and protein. As she settled in at the table, Big Dog dropped a plate piled with food and two longnecks onto the table, before hooking a chair leg with his foot and setting down opposite from her.

"So tell me, what insight did you get into Knight's future, and don't say nothing. The old President of the Chiefs had the same kind of talent that you are gifted with. He would get a vision, and afterwards, shake his head." He'd surprised her with his acceptance of her 'sight'. That made him grin, "We always knew when he had to reboot or whatever you spooky people call it. Why do you think no one has asked you to do your, what did you call it? Party shows?" She was turning light pink and he couldn't help himself, he continued to tease her. "That was why his handle was the Medicine Man. I shit you not, the fact he had a serious love affair with Horse was legendary. He would have visions in the middle of the night that made him scream and yell like someone was killing his ass. He must have been onto something there though, from the time he took office, until the day he OD'd, the club always knew what the other clubs were up to. All he had to do was stand close to one of them."

Future watched him devour his food. He didn't shovel his food into his mouth like some of the men she'd seen over the years, and she enjoyed his conversation. "So it is true what they say about some bikers, they are a superstitious bunch. It wasn't just Merlin and Doobie, and the other guys being assholes.

"When I was younger, they would try to force me to act like a trick pony, Merlin tried everything to develop my abilities. It used to frustrate him to no end when I couldn't read everyone that came in my path. I wasn't allowed to play like a kid. Not that many of the kids around here at the time would have played with me. They mostly looked at me like I was going to tattle on them for everything they did. So they stayed away."

The conversation continued to flow easily, until he apologized for having to go. "I got Church in fifteen minutes. Are you staying here?"

"No, if you don't mind I want to stop in and see my mother while Merlin is out. There something about them that I can't quite put my finger on. I'm hoping she'll open up if it's just me and her."

They parted ways at the front of the building. Seeing her bike parked out front made her smile. At least there wouldn't be another argument when it was time for her to leave in the morning. She had been away from the bar far too long already. If he'd remained stubborn, she might have had to borrow Merlin's old Triumph, or take a bus home.

Her mother didn't have a lot to say at first. "Look, Mom, I know something's bugging you, and I don't want to interfere, but maybe I can help, it doesn't hurt to talk about it right?"

Muffy Smith was still as fluff brained as she'd ever been. Future's mother was always being mistaken for a woman that was considered a few bricks shy of a load, but in reality, she was frightfully intelligent. Muffy had velcro closed tennis shoes, wore her hair in a messy bun at the top of her head, and couldn't understand basic instructions to walk and chew gum at the same time. However, give the woman a computer, and she was in her element. Merlin had no idea the checks that came to his wife each month were royalty checks and paychecks for her computer programming business. All he'd ever said was, he had a sugar momma, and as long as she could afford his drug habit, he was happy to leave her alone with her computers. His attempts at exploiting Future/Oracle were his way of being important.

Muffy wrung her hands and drifted them over her keyboard, before making up her mind to tell her what was going on. "I've decided to leave Merlin. He isn't the man I shack with anymore. All he cares about is his pills and smoking weed. I have been working to try to put money aside so we could retire somewhere warm with a beach.

"I checked my bank account. Merlin has used almost a half of a million dollars over the years for his drug habits, and his lover, did you know that? I have less than ten thousand dollars left in the bank." She looked at her daughter's shocked expression, and saw that she had Oracle's full attention. "I probably should start from the beginning." She sighed, and began her tale. "Merlin and I were best friends, we became roommates years ago. I always knew he was gay, but in those days, they didn't come out of the closet like they do nowadays. Anyway, I was a bit wild you know. He was crazy about motorcycles and wanted to join a gang because he liked the life. I took a few lovers, but never found my Mr. Right. When I found out I was pregnant with you, it was like I'd found my true purpose in life.

"Merlin had parted ways with his lover and we decided to raise you together. Kids should have both a mother and a father you know. I'm sorry I let him use you as a way to be important in the club, my dear. It kept him out of my hair so I could work on my equations and programs, and you were so young that I didn't think you minded the extra attention. I wasn't much of a mother, I see that now. It wasn't until you went missing that I realized how isolated you must have felt.

"When you didn't come back, Merlin began taking more drugs. I expected that your friends would come around asking if there was any word about you." She looked up at Future and there were tears now in both of their eyes. "I couldn't believe no one asked, no young women showed up to ask. At the club, no one spoke your name, like you had never been there. It made me mad, and I was certain you were alive, and no one cared but me.

"I decided I was going to hire a Nomad like Demon to find you. Merlin didn't want to waste the money, and when I saw my account, I found out why. He bought a new bike for his lover. On the weekends, when he swore he was looking for your body, or some real proof that you were dead or alive, he'd been in a hotel room shacked up with his boyfriend using the money I've earned."

She wiped at her eyes, "I could have gotten Big Dog to send Knight or Demon to find you, if I had any idea where to look. I would have to reimburse the club for the use of their resources, but that didn't matter. Having you back is what matters and I just wish you'd contacted me and let me know you were alive. I am having a very hard time forgiving you for leaving me to think you might be dead. I know we weren't the best parents in the world, but we love you."

"Mom, I left and stayed gone because I was betrayed by the club. Or I thought I had been at the time. Even dad was always setting me up like a circus act. If he knew I was alive and still able to speak, he would move heaven and earth to drag me back here so he could keep his status as the handler of the psychic witch. I hated it, I hated all of it. I still won't use my ability unless I have no choice.

"It would be so easy to sell the bar and come back here, especially now that, well you might as well hear it from me first. I had a sex session with Big Dog, and some well meaning asshole will tell you anyway. He isn't going to be easy to forget. I feel things for him that I never expected to have in my life and touching him, I know he feels the same.

We work, even when we shouldn't, and deep down in each of us is a need that when we are together, it's filled. I've dealt with strange shit my whole life but I have to say, what I feel for him, it came out of nowhere. But neither of us has mentioned any long term relationship plans." Her mother didn't appear to be surprised, and all she did was nod her head.

Future was beyond shocked, her parents, who she'd always seen as supportive of each other, were total opposites, and to find out that Merlin was gay, was completely out of left field. Her mother appeared to be waiting for her to say something, but what could she say? Merlin's betrayals were more than a grieving mother should be forced to live with. His theft of her life savings to finance his habits and current partner were past contemptible?

"All right, Mother, what do you want to do, and when do you want to do it? You are certainly welcome to come and stay with me. My house isn't fancy, but it's more than big enough for the two of us. You can even have your own office there, and I promise, you won't have to worry about me draining your bank account. I make a decent living at the bar."

They talked through most of the night. Merlin never showed and since her mother didn't seem concerned, she didn't question his absence. They decided that Muffy would begin packing her personal belongings and arranging the cabin for Merlin's occupancy only. She wasn't going to leave him penniless, but after the five thousand she would be leaving him was gone, he would be on his own. "There is only the ten thousand in this account, and that is all he knows about, thankfully I made arrangements for the new account to be used for electronic payments to be transferred to, so he has no clue, especially now that I sold my latest software program. The technology is advancing so fast that I have been working ten hours a week, just to keep up."

*****

Future woke feeling mentally fit, there was no lingering haze of her usual restless sleeping habits, and although she missed the feelings that Big Dog had left her body with yesterday, it was probably better they make a clean break of things. There had been no promises or demands for a deeper relationship with him. She owed him for showing her that she didn't have to have intense pain to orgasm, and she owed him for the trust he'd placed in her word. Saying goodbye to him would be tough, but she had a life elsewhere, and he had his own responsibilities here. She wondered what she would do if he asked her to stay, as independent as she was, becoming a secondary priority to a man with no promises of mutual love between the two of them would never work. She couldn't reach his deepest feelings as she could with others, they were locked against her touch, only allowing her the slightest peek. And with harden men like Big Dog, it's not easy to know where you stand. Plus, she couldn't just walk away from the bar. Well, she could, but not without some assurances of his feelings for her. For knowing a man only few days, she was way too involved.

Her mother must have thrown the lightweight blanket over her sleeping body, and it gave her a warm feeling. That was a typical mom gesture. She hadn't realized she had missed those small things, until now.

They had bagels and coffee for breakfast, and Future promised to return in two weeks with a moving van and help her mother move her things to her house.

Future walked back to the club, she needed to get her saddlebags, and say goodbye to Big Dog and a few others that had felt comfortable enough to say hello. There was a feeling of hollowness inside of her at the thought of leaving the big man that she hadn't expected to feel.

Little Kevin was running around outside with two of his friends, dodging between the bikes in the parking lot with guns that shot sponge missiles. The sight of the kids playing made her smile, but knowing that some of those bikes had guns hidden in saddlebags, under seats and strapped to the bikes in different areas, gave her visions of death, bloody death. The vision stopped her from moving and when Kevin ran into her, she held onto him and called the other two boys over. She saw a biker that looked familiar, and alarm ran over her sensors. He was a threat. He was still far enough away that she might be able to make it to the safety of the building, but with the three boys, she didn't dare chance a run for it. She bent over Kevin and his two friends came closer.

"I see you are playing war out here, but it's not as good a place as the trees out back. I want you guys to be good at sneaking up on each other and your enemy, so I want you to crawl through the bikes right there." She pointed to the line of bikes in the next to last row. "You keep crawling, stay down until you reach the gate, you're lucky I can see that its open right now, or the enemy would hear it squeak. When you have cleared the gate, run into the trees and stay there hiding from the enemy until me or Knight comes to find you. Can you do that?" They all nodded and she pretended to time them by looking at her phone's clock. "Okay, men, no matter what you hear, carry out your mission."

There was only twenty-five feet from where they dropped to their knees and began to crawl, until they reached the gate, and safety. She kept the man in her sight, as she moved through the sea of bikes. He started moving faster, and she sped up her steps. She saw a bike in front of her and eyed the bulging bag hanging over the rear fender. She dropped down to reach in the bag, and found nothing but clothing, and a plastic bag filled with herb.

She popped her head up and the guy took a shot at her, narrowly missing the gas tank of a rat bike. She ran toward the entrance of the building, now that she'd drawn him away from the boys. She knew he was too close for her to reach safety, and stayed crouched behind the Boss Hoss that sat in the front row, with its customized trunk that contained a rumble seat that was rarely used. The sidecar was a miniature version of a 1970s Boss Mustang. Both were painted mirror black with silver stripes and lots of chrome. The club owned the thing, and fondly called it the Limo.

She could hear him calling out to her, trying to strike terror into her, he had to know she was trying to wait him out. And when she heard his step directly behind her, she knew her time had run out. He lifted his foot and connected with her shoulder to knock her down.

Seeing that her assailant was Dorsey's buddy, Krebs, didn't surprise her. Dorsey would be too cowardly to attempt something this stupid. He raised the gun and said, "You shoulda' stayed dead, bitch." She kicked her leg up as the gun went off. The toe of her foot connected with his knee, and he lurched to the side. The rocks next to her stomach kicked up, but he didn't get another shot off. There was a throwing knife sticking out of his neck, and his eyes were raised to see who the knife belonged to. She didn't bother to look, his fingers were beginning to tighten on the gun and she kicked his kneecap with everything she could and he yelled, then as he started to fall, he squeezed the trigger again and gurgled blood when the bullet hit his foot. She rolled away from his falling body, getting out of the way for the men who descended on them.

Crazy Charlie pulled her by the arm and bent to help her stand. She was fine, there were a few scratches from the sharp rocks cutting her arm, but she was alright. "That was a good throw with the dagger, thank you." He nodded and looked to where the body of Krebs was lying.

"I'm going home, this is getting dangerous for me around here. He was with Dorsey that night of the attack, and he just told me I should have stayed dead. Dorsey is a chicken shit coward, and he will never show his face when other people might be around." She asked him to find the children and make sure they were safe. "You might want to let their parents know they were playing out here between the bikes."

Charlie agreed with her. "Those little critters aren't 'sposed to be out here anyway. I know for a fact they've been told not to be out front. So there's gonna be some sore asses by bedtime unless I miss my guess."

She didn't see Big Dog before she left. He hadn't been at the club or in his side of the duplex when she retrieved her saddlebags and clothes from his place. Butch stopped her on her way to the door.

"Where do you think you're going, Future? Nobody told me you were leaving."

She wasn't in the mood for the macho shit she knew he liked to lecture about. Butch was a great guy to have at your back in a fight. He was smart, and his wife was beautiful. He was also a chauvinist down to his toenails.

"Big Dog gave me my ride back, it's right out front in the lot, and I have a business to run at home. I did everything that was asked of me, and now it's time to leave."

When he shook his head, she was afraid he was going to ground her to the club, but he told her to wait a few minutes and left the room. Fifteen minutes later, he came back with Freakshow and a new patch they called Larry.

"The boys will ride with you to keep you company. I'm warning you right now in front of them, if you try to ditch them, they're gonna call me or Big Dog, and you will not like what happens then. You feel me?"

Chapter Nine

The ride home was uneventful. They spent the night in a cozy mom and pop motor inn lodge that had to have been in use since the Fifties. The sheets were clean and the bathrooms spotless. There was cable television, but Future was too tired to bother watching the news. Freakshow and Larry called for takeout pizza and they ate in her room. They talked about Larry's family and his brother who was serving time for armed robbery. Larry came from Fresno. He had a small speech impediment, but when he slowed down, he spoke clearly enough to understand what he was saying. He was a nice guy that wanted a place to belong, and the Bastards was the place he decided to stay.

Freakshow told her she could call him Mathew on the road. "My mother is a strict Catholic and wanted me to be a priest. My father wanted me to leave home, so I wouldn't embarrass him because of my tats and the gauged ears."

They talked about all kinds of things, and she worried at first that Mathew would mention her scars, but he never did. She told them they could stay at her place for a day or two if they wanted to look around the city, and even invited them to come to the bar and she would introduce them to a few ladies if they were interested. That offer got big grins from both men. They went to their room and she promised to wake them if she decided to leave early.

She might have only slept with Big Dog, actually slept with him for a few hours, but she missed the warmth and comfort of his body lying next to hers. She was sorry that he wasn't at the club when she was ready to leave because she had plans for that body of his. Unfortunately, she was deprived of his company, and had he known it, he was deprived of her plans to have his prick in her mouth for a going away, thank you kind of gift.

At five a.m. she was ready to go. She tried watching the news, but seeing the rescue people recovering the body of a long time drug user with ties to the Burning Bastards Motorcycle Club from the trash dumpster behind City Hall, made her shudder. Krebs was a lousy excuse for a human being to begin with, to feel only relief at the death of another human being made her what? Human? Knowing there was one who deserved death even more, made her shut the news off and wake up the men.

If they pushed it, they could be at her place before ten tonight.

They got to the bar at ten thirty, and she opened the delivery door in back of the building so they could all park their bikes inside for the night. They walked through the back lot and she unlocked the gate for them to walk through her backyard to the house. The place impressed Mathew and he praised the setup.

"It's cool. You got a great place here. It would make a cool clubhouse too."

She laughed at his enthusiasm. "No way, you guys would drink up all my profits, and I'd be panhandling on a street corner to pay the mortgage. Not to mention, my mother is going to come live with me in a couple of weeks. She is planning to turn one of the bedrooms into her very own computer heaven."

They'd stopped for a quick dinner on the way home, so she showed them the two spare rooms that had beds. One was a bit on the frilly side but she gave them the choice of who would bunk in where. "You two hash it out, the bathrooms across the hall between the rooms, so I think that's probably all you might need for the night. There is frozen dinners in the freezer and soft drinks in the fridge if you get hungry or thirsty. Help yourselves."

At midnight her phone played its silly little tune and she glanced at the number before accepting the call. His voice made her smile, even as he bitched at her for leaving without saying goodbye. "What the hell, Future, you don't just walk away after the things we did woman. I was in court for Kevin, Butch said he didn't think it was your business, so he didn't tell you where I was. I figured we'd have more time to get to know each other better. I'm more than a sex object you know. I even own a home, a goat that mows the lawn at the house, and a big damn hive of yellow jackets in the backyard that I can't get near enough to burn out yet."

She couldn't help it, she laughed, "You're a regular citizen there. Tell me, what would the world think if they knew the president of the badassed bikers was a taxpaying homeowner? I heard Seth talking to Tiny about a semi truck repair shop by the way. Since I passed it at the interchange on the highway ramp, I thought the name Big Dog's Diesel was kinda catchy. Looks legit to me."

When he didn't laugh, instead staying silent, she sighed and continued.

"I needed to get back to the bar, Clem was having issues with personnel, and I have to deal with it tomorrow."

"Dammit, when they told me about Krebs. I wanted to kill the fucker myself."

Their conversation lasted through the next two hours. He told her to, "Keep it warm for me, I'll be visiting as soon as I can get away. Oh, and if Show or Larry touched you, I'm going to kill them. I don't share my guns, my bank account, or my woman unless I am there at the time. Remember it."

They said their goodbyes and she laid her phone on the bedside table. A single tear slid down her cheek as she rolled to her side, grabbing the extra pillow and squeezed it tight, missing him already.

*****

She was awake by six a.m. and dragging ass around the kitchen, making coffee, and trying to figure out what she had on hand to fix for breakfast. Eggs, cheese, and some frozen sausage patties that she didn't remember buying were in the freezer.

She was listening to the morning news when Mathew came in the room. He had a couple of sheets of drawing paper in his hand, and handed them to her as he passed by her chair on his way to the coffeepot.

At first glance, she was embarrassed that he'd remembered what her back looked like. As her eyes traveled down the first page, she could see her crude scars were being transformed into a beautiful scene.

The area under the ravaged melted wing depicted a bike, with more bikes in a progression of smaller images, until it appeared the wing covered and protected a sea of motorcycles. Above the word 'FALLEN', as the word 'THE', and the 'AN', was completed in ink as 'ANGEL'. 'FALLEN' had a colon and an S added. For the words 'THE FALLEN'S ANGEL'. The scene was color coded, with notations, and she knew she had to have this done. The scars were ugly, yet they could be used as a rough sketch for a good tattoo artist. Her fingers followed each line and she thought of the possibilities.

"Sorry about that, but I kept seeing that melted wing in my mind, and I've known about your rep for helping out the club over the years. It seemed to fit, you know?"

It choked her up. This strange man with a talent to be able to see beauty in something so ugly, amazed her. She nodded her head and did her best to listen to the idea that he started talking about to use the scars as a bare bones start.

"We can put the club's logo between the lines on your ribs too if you want." He took the papers, and started sketching more amazing ways to hide or play up the scars. "The effect when you move will be A-fucking awesome. If I can get it right, it will have a three dimensional appearance, and when you move it will look like the wings are folding over the bikers."

They discussed his reasons for not showing off his talent as an artist before now, and he shrugged his shoulders. "The guys go to the place in town, and if I wanted to open an ink shop I'd have to start out with customers waiting. I used to work at the Ink Shack and did pretty good before the blow up with my old man. How many people want tattoos from an unknown artist? Not to mention, I don't have the money to open a business like that."

She thought about his valid reasoning, after all, opening your own business did take money, even something as small scale as he would need would take a few grand to start. She might be wasting her money, and her back might end up looking like shit, but he couldn't mess it up worse than it already was, so she made her decision.

"I'll give you my credit card, and my truck, and you find a place where you can purchase what you need to make these sketches into reality. You can keep the equipment when you're finished in payment. And, if it comes out as beautiful as these drawings promise. I'll let you take a picture to use for advertisement. Just the tattoos, not my face, or the other places with scars."

Larry wandered in and she made them help fix breakfast when he bragged about his omelet making abilities. She gave over the keys to the truck, a spare key to the house, and her credit card. She wasn't worried they would steal from her, if they did, they were facing a far harsher punishment than any judge would give to them. You don't steal from a member, you can ask for, or receive help when it was needed, but you never steal.

She waited for them to leave, and took the tunnel entrance to the bar. Everything looked good from what she could see. Hearing Wanda screech out John's name in the quiet of the place made her jump, until she realized what the screams actually were. "Fuck me harder, you fat son-of-a-bitch," was not her idea of talking to a lover, but then she had to admit, John did have a considerable gut. The last time she'd heard the two middle-aged lovers going at it, they were having oral sex on the fake leather couch in her office. "Eat me, and swallow it all," gave her a mental picture that had refused to go away for weeks.

This morning she envied their relationship. Enjoying sex at work was a safe way of enjoying the forbidden; after all, the probability of being discovered was low. They worked together as a team when the bar was closed. She had never let on that she knew they were using the bar as a trysting place. Wanda was married to a man who was paralyzed and lived in a nursing facility. She refused to divorce her husband of thirty years, saying she couldn't abandon the man who'd fathered her children before his accident. John was closed mouth about his personal life to Future, she knew almost nothing about the man, other than he seemed to care about Wanda.

She went back to the house to make a shopping list. It would take Mathew a few days to do her tattoo, and she knew Larry would stick close too. One of them had better be able to cook more than eggs, or they'd be eating a lot of takeout. She had to

106

be at the bar most nights, especially since she'd been absent these past few days.

Future texted the list to Mathew's cell phone. He had her card and could purchase what they needed so she wouldn't have to take the time to do it herself when they came back with her truck. Having them around would be good preparation for living with her mother ghosting around the house.

*****

The Big Dog was in a rotten mood and everyone noticed it. The morning of the attempt on Future's life, he was stuck in court swearing that Kevin was more than welcome in his home and that he could and did provide a safe, sanitary, and secure home filled with love for Kevin's needs. The Guardian at Litem argued that Hugh was the President of an Outlaw Motorcycle Group, and therefore suspect as a fit parent for a young impressionable mind. She further asked the court to reconsider placement of Kevin to a state approved Foster Home until the court could determine his permanent home. The Suits countered that Hugh had no criminal history, and wasn't a suspect in any ongoing cases of a legal matter. He was also the child's only living relative. Therefore, he should be allowed to keep Kevin as his own child.

Had he known the child advocate would be such a fucking cunt about it, he would have taken care of her before the hearing. She was an uptight spinster with her brown hair in a bun and thick glasses who wore a pencil skirt suit, and a sour expression. He was determined to either change her mind, or find a way to make her change her mind. If she disappeared now, he would be a suspect, but he wasn't the kind of man to harm a woman, physically anyway.

The Suits had won for now, pending the investigation of Hugh's residence and living arrangements.

He'd no more gotten back to the club when he was greeted with the news of Kreb's screwed up attempt at assassinating Future. Charlie and Butch assured him that she was fine, with only superficial cuts on her arm, there wasn't anything to stress about.

Butch set his mind at ease with the news that he'd sent Freakshow and Larry with her for protection. "Look, man, I had no reason to keep her here, and who wants a pissed off psychic hanging around bitching that she needed to get home to her life. I told her not to ditch the guys, or else."

When Larry called two days later, and told Butch that they would be staying for a few more days to do some sightseeing, it caused Big Dog a few restless hours of sleep. Was she letting them fuck her? He couldn't believe that would happen, she needed a man, not a kid, or a guy that got his jollies from seeing how far he could stretch his earlobe. No, there must be some other reason for their prolonged stay. He called her at two in the morning, she was just closing the bar and promised to call him back as soon as she got home. Her "I miss you" went a long way to reassure him that she wasn't fucking another man, he trusted her. *Right? Yeah, he trusted her, but what about Show, he was attractive to some women, no, Show wasn't that stupid.* His thoughts calmed down when he realized that he was acting like a jealous asshole. He didn't own her. Yet.

When she called at three fifteen sounding exhausted, but happy to talk to him, he knew she was being straight with him. He felt a kick to his gut each time she said, "I miss you." He needed to do something about the two of them. This long distance shit was just that, shit.

The Sheriff's deputies came that morning to inform him that one of his members had been found in the dumpster behind City Hall, so he had to act concerned. Who would do such a heinous thing? He asked about surveillance videos and all the appropriate questions a concerned friend would ask, but it got them redirected at the gangs that had begun to crop up in small towns lately. Let them feel some heat for once. The cops were so busy watching the bikers that they'd forgotten about the city gangs. At least bikers didn't steal old ladies purses and cut up pets to pretend they were badasses or Devil worshippers.

The old farmhouse that sat back off the road, with sixty acres and a big pole barn, was only a half a mile from the clubhouse, and Big Dog had been renovating it for over a year in his spare time. He used the place as his home address on the court papers, and knew he needed to finish up at least two of the four bedrooms in the house before that Ms. Pearson showed up to check on the living conditions at his home. He drafted Charlie and a few of the greybeards to help him since they didn't have day jobs, and the old house was shaping up fine. As luck would have it, Ms. Pearson showed up while he was at Kevin's school for a conference with the teacher concerning the boy's inattention to his homework.

Charlie gave her the tour and showed her the plans that Hugh had drawn up for the property. While he was at it, he got her chatting about her life and they were talking like old friends before he was finished with the tour. She asked him about the club and he offered to take her for a ride on his bike the next day, which just happened to be Saturday, and her day off. His brand of rough charm must have worked, especially when she found out how lonely the older man was. "I don't have a lady in my life and I never had any kids to tie me down. This group of people is my family, but it's still lonely, if you know what I mean." He walked her around the outside of the house once more, and took her elbow so she wouldn't stumble on the uneven ground. She let his hand stay on her arm, even when it was no longer necessary for him to steady her. "Would it be too ignorant of me to ask if you would go for a ride with me tomorrow? I promise not to mention Hugh or Kevin, I know you are a woman with ethics, and I would never try to change your mind about something as important as a child's safety."

He walked her to her car and opened the door for her to sit in the driver's seat. Before he closed the door, she gave him her address and telephone number with a shy smile. He looked at the paper and saw that her first name was Selma, he kinda liked the name Selma.

Chapter Ten

Four days after Future left him, he showed up at the bar. She was tending bar and almost dropped the tray of beers she'd just filled an order for, when he stepped inside, and without hesitation, walked toward her. She put the tray down and hurried to the end of the bar where he was standing, waiting for her. He was so tall that all he had to do was reach over to haul her over the polished wood and into his arms. The catcalls and whoops from her patrons was ignored as he smashed her lips with his, and laid a slap on her ass that everyone in the place could hear. His arms were wrapped so tightly around her that she had to pinch his belly to have him allow her to draw air into her lungs. His, "You'll pay for that," and his not so quiet demand to show him her office, gave her a thrill. "Either you show me a private spot in this place, or I'll fuck you right here."

The yells and clapping was strange to hear, even in the bar that had grown so popular since she'd purchased the place, that she hid her face in his chest. "The back room where my office is has a couch." He kept his hold around her, and carried her into the hallway until they came to the door with Office written on it, and he set her down long enough to open the door and push her inside.

"You left without saying goodbye. Imagine my surprise when I got back from court about Kevin and you were gone. Not only are you gone, but there was a dead Krebs to take care of and Butch barely avoided being beaten to death by sending the men with you." His words were accompanied by his busy hands removing her clothing. "You have some making up to do, woman."

When he'd left yesterday, he told himself that he was just coming here to see what his men were doing. All week he'd been horny and grouchy, but even the fluffers, women who show up at the club on weekends to walk on the wild side, doing anything and everything asked of them but not looking for a love connection, didn't hold any appeal for him. He wanted his scarred Future. It didn't make any sense and he didn't give a shit. She was the one his prick wanted and as far as he was concerned, that was that. Now that his emotions were involved, fucking her out of his system wasn't going to work like he'd thought it would.

She went to her knees in front of him before he could tell her what he wanted and had her hands on his belt and the button of his jeans. Once she'd sprung his prick from the confines of his pants, she looked up at him and smiled. "Let me see if I can apologize in a way that will make an impression. I've been fantasizing about this since the morning I woke and you were gone. I planned to do this as a parting gift you know, now just enjoy, and tell me if I'm doing this wrong." She began to lick his prick on the head and slowly made her way to the root of the shaft. Her hand kept a hold of his eager prick as she slid her mouth over the entire head and began to draw him inside with only the suction of her mouth. One of her hands scratched the tight wrinkles of his sac, and a wandering fingernail scraped his taint.

His hands grabbed fistfuls of her hair and she made a humming sound that went straight through his cock to his already heated balls. She curled the finger teasing his taint and pushed her knuckle up, stretching the skin, and making him feel the euphoria of the sperm rushing to his prick. "Dammit, I'm coming, damn you, I—take it, oh yeah, take it all, let me feel your throat, yeah. Like that." His semen shot into the back of her throat and coated every crevice of her mouth. He could feel her attempts to swallow as fast as his liquid offering filled her mouth and he jerked as she continued to suck until he had given all he could for the time being. When she made a chewing motion on his sensitive head, he pulled out of her mouth with a quick motion of his hips.

He pulled up with his hands still fisted in her hair. She stood and he pulled her head back to gain access to her mouth, neck, and shoulders, for his teasing kisses. She was breathing heavily by the time he came up for air. He turned her and pushed her over the high back of the couch, hoisting her hips a bit for the angle he wanted, when he stopped to look at her back. "Well I'll be damned, this is fucking beautiful. Flex your shoulders again, I swear it looks like the wings are folding over the bikes. That's impressive, I love this. I really like the logo too." His fingers traced her newly colored tattoo on the outside of the lines, because the tat was still pink and healing. He'd had plenty of experience with getting new ink, and knew enough not to disturb the art until it was healed. "I don't know who your artist is, but I want to see if they will do my next tat. This is a real work of art."

Where women normally had a tramp stamp put over the cracks of their asses was the Burning Bastards logo. A skeleton standing in a circle of flames with the ring depicting a speedometer looking at the viewer, and flipping the bird was depicted on her lower back. The small jagged scars on her thighs were now rain clouds and when he pulled her up to see the front of her belly and ribs, long zig-zags of lightning bolts ran across the expanse. "I never thought to use the raised skin to create such effects in a tattoo. All I can say is damn."

"I think you will be surprised when I tell you that Matthew is the artist. I am so pleased with the results that I plan to bankroll him when he finds a place to open shop. It was his idea to make the angel into a security thing, and he came up with the rest too. I had the witch hat and the symbol on my neck done when I was eighteen."

His, "Matthew who?" made her smile. "Matthew, known at the crib as Freakshow. He was at the meeting and saw my scars, he showed me some sketches of things he thought could be done to make the ugly things into what you see. I admit to being teary eyed each time he finishes another one. It took him four days to get my tats just right. The man has a wicked fast imagination."

She found herself back into the original position that he'd put her in over the couch's back. Two of his long fingers slid easily into her wet tunnel, and she gasped as he worked the fingers hard and fast inside.

His fingers left her begging for more, but he replaced them with his thick cock and slammed inside her as hard as he dared. The idea that Freakshow had seen her mostly naked in order to complete those beautiful tattoos pissed him off. He kept up his harsh pace until he felt her channel contract around his prick. He knew he would hose her pussy until she was filled completely with his flesh and semen and the idea added to his excitement, he reached around her to rub her unprotected clit with his fingers. The unearthly noise that came from between her clenched teeth, and the way her pussy clamped down on his cock as it attempted to squeeze and suction the come from his balls and prick, blew his control completely.

When they got their breath back, they went into the bar where the patrons cheered them. He sat on the stool where the bar ended at the wall and grinned when three beers were set in front of him by the woman they called Clem. "You have a fan club, a few of the men who've been hitting on Future for a while now and getting nowhere fast, sent these. One of them said to tell you that you must be a hell of a man to take that witch on." She eyed him up and down, "I gotta say I tend to agree with him." She smiled at him and went about her business.

At one thirty in the morning, Larry and Freakshow walked into the bar and saw their President sitting by himself, so they joined him. Larry stood back a bit, still nervous around the big man. Eventually, he became comfortable, but still remained cautious with his words. Even when Big Dog mentioned the tattoos that he'd seen on Future's skin.

"I couldn't believe it when she flexed her shoulders, that angel looked like she was moving— that was cool as hell, man. Good work. Now you can tell me why you've been sandbagging it, working in the body shop when you can do work like that on skin. You can set up shop in the same building that Cherry and Kitty have their salon. If you can do work like that, you'll run that fucker Marlow out of business in six months."

He eyed a nervous Larry before asking him what light he was hiding under a bushel.

"I've been finding out all kinds of abilities the Bastards have. I got a hold of Muffy, that's Future's mother FYI. Anyway, I want a list of everyone's hobby's and experience. We need more legit businesses for the books, and something for the elders to do when they retire from the everyday job. I found four greybeards that were builders and carpenters that have made my renovation of the farmhouse a hell of a lot easier. Joker told me that he's old, not dead.

"Larry, you can see Muffy and get the questionnaires and be responsible for talking to the under twenty-five-year-olds. I don't give a shit if they flipped burgers in their teen years, or can hypnotize goats. I want to know what we have for resources. The Bastards need to move with the times.

"I plan on leaving around noon tomorrow, I expect you two are coming with me?" The nods came promptly, even if Larry had his eyes on the pretty dancer that was doing her thing on the small platform with the stainless pole.

By closing time, Larry had stopped stuttering when Big Dog asked him a question. The man had the meanest look on his face most of the time, even when he wasn't frowning, but the more they talked, the less frightened Larry felt. Until the drunk that started yelling at Future and calling her a trashy whore, became the center of Big D's attention. He slowly stood, and a couple of the drunken man's friends saw him and where the big man was focused. They tried to pull him back, but the drunk wasn't moving until he'd had his say.

"Fuckin' cunt. You took that big motherfucker in the back and fucked him, what's wrong with me? My dick probably ain't as big as his is, but I ain't ashamed of it either. A whore like you should be grateful that a man with a job looks at you. You're like all the other cocksucking bitches. You'll lay down for any greasy bad boy looking faggot that comes along."

He was too dumb for words, Future couldn't help but laugh. "He's not greasy, although he is an asshole at times, and he has a prick that's bigger than your drunken ass can imagine. As to him being a faggot. You saw us go into the back room, and I could barely walk straight when we came out, but you can ask him if you'd like. My advice is for you to leave now, while you still can."

"Yeah, well fuck you." He poked his finger her way, "Fuck that fat ass of yours." He was gearing up for another barrage of filthy descriptions for her when he squeaked, his feet were dangling, and his friends backed away. The man was only an inch or so taller than Future was, and that put him over a foot shorter than Big Dog. He was slammed down on a barstool and the big guy slapped him with an open palm to gain his attention.

"You jealous that she gets my cock and you don't? Well, boy, I can stand the smell if you can stand the pain. You just bend that ass over right here and we'll see if you're as good a cocksucker as your mouth looks like it is. In fact, I have a damn good idea." He looked back at his brothers. "His buddies thought it was funny when he was insulting my woman, I bet they'd like to feel this fucker's mouth wrapped around their pricks. Show, invite the boys to take their pants off and sit a while. Funny boy here is going to entertain us." He slapped the dumbass again, a little harder this time.

"You're gonna show us how good that mouth of yours is, aren't you? Nod your stupid head if you understand." The guy began to struggle, but Big Dog slapped him on the head this time. "Boy, you don't seem to comprehend simple English. You are going to suck your friend's cocks, and if you don't, you're going to get ass fucked by three greasy motherfuckers, and when each of us has hosed your asshole, you and your buddies get to clean our cocks with your mouths."

His hand went under the man's chin and lifted his head high enough to stare into his eyes. "You come into a bar on the edge of town in your shiny leather jackets like you're fuckin' slumming in a bar that caters to bikers and rednecks, and try to throw your importance around like we should be impressed. Go suck those cocks, little man, I don't like you and I have no problem going back to prison, some of my best friends are there."

Big Dog let the man drop on his knees, and booted him in the ass. "Don't take all fuckin' night about it."

After his initial reluctance was noted and dealt with by the feel of a blade along his neck, his performance was critiqued by the bikers. Recommendations for him to take the cock in his mouth deeper were ignored, so Larry grabbed a handful of his hair and shoved his head up and down in an acceptable fashion. Kendal and Clementine cheered him on with enthusiastic helpful hints. "You need to flatten your tongue so the prick slides to the back of your throat." Was one piece of advice. "Suck that cock down, it's small enough that you can fit the whole thing in your mouth, he ain't that big."

After each man had squirted his jizz half into his mouth and half on his face, they had to kiss him for giving them so much pleasure. Big Dog took their wallets and made a production of going through them, and let them watch as he jotted down their names and addresses on a paper towel. He kept making comments about the pictures in the wallets, "Show, look at this slut, I bet she'd like to take a ride on your bike." He tossed the wallets at the men after each one had been gone through. The fear on their faces was more than worth the price of admission as far as he was concerned. It had been too long since he'd purposefully scared the shit out of a few golden boys, and it felt good. Larry had taken their cell phones and used the video features to record the kisses, so each man had a reminder of their walk on the wrong side of the tracks.

They made the men get dressed, and even told the stupid little prick to comb his hair before unlocking the door and allowing them to exit the building. "You boys be sure and come back now."

Matthew and Larry walked the girls to their cars and continued through the back gate and into the house.

Future kept giving him strange looks. She shook her head and laughed aloud a few times while she was putting the bar to rights for the night. Rather than walk outside and around in the dark, she led him through the tunnel and he was impressed. They'd no sooner entered the door in the cellar of the house than they could hear a loud booming sound reaching back to them from the way they'd come.

Big Dog shoved her through the door and followed her, before slamming it closed behind them. Future was freaking out and knew it, but she couldn't help herself. "What was that? Dammit, what just happened?" They ran up the steps and looked out of the window in the back door. It looked like a bomb had gone off in the front of the building. She could only stare as he called 911 and gave them the particulars such as location and the name of the business. After assuring the dispatch that no one remained inside the burning business, he hung up the phone and gathered her into his arms, while they watched the building burn.

"The guys' bikes are in there with mine. Shit, I loved that damn bike." The two men came down the stairs at a fast clip and almost ran into the couple standing at the back door, watching the fire. As they all watched, a lone man came out of the shadows and got close to the fire before he fumbled with his pants and appeared to take a leak near the flames. His head snapped up as they all heard the sirens in the distance and melted back into the shadows. Within minutes they saw a bike and its rider slow down as it drove past the burning building.

Future stated what the rest of them already suspected. "Dorsey. That cowardly son-of-a-bitch."

They were standing at the gate to her backyard when the police arrived, and firemen began trying to put the fire out. She walked over to the nearest cop and told him who she was. She told him that she'd just left the building, and everything appeared the same as any other night, "I locked it up and came home through the tunnel between the buildings. No one but the former owner and I know about the tunnel. It was a busy night and the employees had just left before I did. I should probably call them to make sure they find out about it from me, and not on the morning news."

She noticed the back portion of the building wasn't engulfed in flames yet and she grabbed the cop's arm, "You need to tell them that there are three motorcycles in that back room. The gas tanks are full, and that's where I store the cases of whisky and wine."

The cop took off running toward the firemen and she stayed where she was. Big Dog came to her side and slid his arm around her as they watched the progress being made by the firemen on the flames. Every now and then they could hear a small explosion, and the fire would flare for a minute, and drop down again. The officer came back and Big Dog introduced himself as Hugh Dougherty, a good friend of Oracle's.

The sun was shining in the early morning hours as the firemen began rolling their hoses and the police began rolling out the yellow caution tape. Future talked with the cop and asked if there would be any problem if she hired some people to remove the cases of booze from the back room the firemen had managed to save from harm. "I'm just worried some kids will come along and think its Christmas coming early. I don't want to be responsible for any drunken teenagers wandering the streets of the city. The same thing for the bikes, we can bring them through the back gate and I can park them in my garage." The cop thought both points were valid and accompanied them to the storage room to see for himself that she'd been speaking the truth.

He took a quick inventory of the cases of booze and copied the VIN numbers off the bikes before nodding his permission to move the things. After the crowd of cops and firemen left, Larry and Matthew rolled the bikes into her garage, parking them next to Big Dog's hog.

The men shuttled the cases of whiskey and wine into the garage too. Her truck was now a driveway dweller, but that would be all right because once the men left, she would have more than enough room to park the small truck in the space left open.

Chapter Eleven

She was so tired that after she showered, she dropped her towel next to her bed and pulled back the covers, intending to sleep for the next four hours. Instead, she sat down and pulled a pillow into her lap, buried her face in the pillow, and cried her heart out.

*****

"Hey, Big D. I called a few people I know, well they are actually my brother's best friends." Larry was back to being intimidated, but Big D, as the smaller man tagged him, was in no mood for patience today.

"Larry, I don't mind the tag, in fact I like it, but just spit it out. I don't have time for your nerves right now."

Larry took that as a direct order. "I called Jerome and Eduardo. I figured if anyone can find a rat like Dorsey, well, it takes a thief to catch a thief, you know?" Seeing the look on Big D's face, he hurried with his news. "Eduardo said that an old guy on a big bike was seen by some of their friends when he came looking for some C-4, and a quarter pound of weed. He paid in gold chains, like real gold I mean. And this morning, this old guy, he was seen heading out of town, going west."

His information earned him a pat on the back and a "good job." It made him feel good.

Freakshow was methodically tossing a dagger at a small square of wood he'd found in the garage. Larry left him alone, no way did he want to further piss off the man with the pointy knife, so he took his ass to bed, knowing they'd be riding in a few short hours.

Big Dog was on the phone talking to Butch. "I want that motherfucker, he was seen traveling west, so he might be heading back to the crib, and he might have more C-4, we don't know how much he bought. Get the kids out of there, take them to the farm. They can camp out for the weekend. We'll be leaving here as soon as I get a couple of hours of sleep."

He took a quick shower and found Future lying on her side with a pillow in her arms and trails of dried tears on her cheeks. He pulled the pillow from her arms and rolled her over to cuddle her close. The tears disturbed him more than they should. She was stronger than any woman he'd met, but if she was going to cry, he guessed she had a good reason. Knowing they'd been so close to blowing up in that building put a lot of things in perspective for him. For now, he needed to rest.

*****

Matthew Douglas signed the note he left at the house before he left.

Couldn't sleep, going to follow up on a few things and will meet you at the crib.

Everything was packed in his saddlebags and he left the house locked up. There were a few places he wanted to check before heading to the club; one of them happened to be an hour's ride from there. His mind was now calm, it was surprising how he could find serenity during chaos, but it worked for him, and that's what mattered after all was said and done.

The woman that answered the door to his knock was older than he remembered her to be, her hair was an unnatural shade of light brown for a woman in her sixties, and she stared at him as if seeing a ghost. "Matthew? Is that really you?" She reached out her hand to his cheek and cradled his jaw in her open palm. It had been twelve years since he'd walked out of the door, and never looked back before today.

She pulled his arm to lead him into the house that he'd grown up in. Other than new paint, and a few newer pieces of furniture, nothing had changed in the place since he was here last. He sat in the kitchen and she fluttered around the room until she got the coffee and heated the apple muffins with cream cheese icing laces drizzled over the top. He hadn't said anything and waited for her to sit on a chair.

After the preliminaries and having her tell him that his father, who had, in fact, been a stepfather, had died from a heart attack five years ago. She was now a widow, and was thinking about a move to Florida or Texas. "So what brings you to my door, son? I have been writing letters for years trying to get you to come visit me, but my letters come back to me. Paul told me to stop bothering, that you were too bitter and refused to consider that I might want to reconnect with my son. I tried to only send cards and food gift certificates, and I still have half of them in the drawer I keep your letters in. Each time one would be returned, it hurt. Thank you for coming today"

Over the next three hours, he learned that Paul was living here with his mother. He had been living with her for the past two months or so. "He lost his job, and needed a place to stay until he could find regular work."

Paul was his father's stepbrother. Paul had "done his brother a favor" by fathering a child with the brother's wife when the brother hadn't been up to the challenge. That made sense now, the man he'd always thought was his father, was actually his stepfather, and Paul Dorsey was his biological father.

After the last blow up that had ended with his father giving him a week to get out of his house, and overhearing his father telling his mother how worthless her son was. He'd almost missed the truth when the man said that Paul had fathered rotten fruit, and he was sick of the pansy assed little fucker taking up space and eating the food he provided. "Let Paul provide for his bastard."

Mathew had packed a small duffel with two changes of clothes, rolled his duster and the few valuables he owned, and left on his Triumph Trident 750—he still owned that bike. It took five years for him to find a home with the Bastards. He remembered the hell he'd gone through to get to that point and hoped that he never had a kid that ended up like he did, until he found the group. Now he knew he wanted a couple of kids in the future. He still had time enough to pick a decent woman who was ready for a relationship.

126

One day he was in the game room at the club, and saw someone vaguely familiar. When he heard the name Paul, he paid attention, even if there were thousands of men named Paul in the world. That night, he waited until most of the guys were asleep, and slipped around to the man's bike and found the proof he needed. The hog was registered to Paul Dorsey, his biological father.

The day Future had to testify in front of him and the other five men drove the knowledge into him that the fucker needed to die. He hated the thought of being forced to tell anyone the man was related to him, so he was going to take care of the fucker once and for all if he could find him. That was why he'd come to his mother's door. She had choices during her years of marriage to the abusive bastard. She could have taken him and left her husband. She could have refused to allow her husband's stepbrother to fuck her in the first place. She could have let Mathew beat the bastards head in the night he broke her cheekbone and sprained her ankle when she went down. She chose to stay, and he freely admitted that he loved his mother, but he felt zero respect for her life choices.

Now it appeared that Paul left sometime last evening to take a job in California. He didn't say when he was coming back, but she figured it wouldn't be long before he sent for the boxes of his things that were sitting in the spare bedroom. "There's only three of them, and they're not very large, but he said they were important to him, and would I make sure they were kept safe."

He agreed to stay the night and she decided to go to the store for something special to cook for dinner. He told her he needed a nap if that was all right with her, and she smiled in motherly concern. "Well, I will take my time at the store so you can have a nice sleep."

As soon as she cleared the driveway, he slit the tape on the boxes and discovered how important the contents actually were. The first box solved the mystery of the way Dorsey had paid the gangbangers in gold. There was thousands of dollars worth of gold and platinum jewelry in the box. Some of the rings held stones, but all of the stuff was real, even the men's watches that sold in the store for two to five grand each.

Matthew took the box and upended it into a doubled plastic grocery bag, and placed the bag in the bottom of his saddlebag. He re-taped the empty box, and moved on to the next one. It contained notebooks filled with information on several of the Bastards and a few newer ones on the hierarchy of Lucifer's Breed. He didn't have time to go through them all, so they went into the saddlebags too. The third box was a bit larger than the first two had been, and when he opened the box, what he found creeped him out.

In the folds of shirts and jeans, were small boxes of teeth. There were only four of them, and a box containing dryer sheets and blackened fingertips. Matthew knew he'd found Paul Dorsey's trophy stash. He went to his mother's laundry room and grabbed a few dryer sheets and dampened them, before going through the box again, wiping his fingerprints from every surface that he'd touched. He re-taped the box, making certain his prints were not on the sticky side of the tape, and gave the entire box the same treatment that he gave the contents. No way did he want his prints on something like this. Nor did he want to leave it in his mother's home.

He took a quick two hour nap, and woke to the scent of something that made his stomach rumble. Going out to the kitchen, he found her taking a pan of lasagna out of the oven. She must have remembered that her lasagna was his favorite meal while he lived at home. Since he'd left, he avoided the stuff from anywhere else. It was his way of remembering something good from his childhood. The same thing with her Chicken Noodle soup; on a cold day, or when anyone caught a cold, she made soup. He had many people and places tempt him into trying the soups, but it wasn't his mother's, so he refused to touch it. *I guess I'm more fucked up than I realized.*

He watched the nighttime game shows with her and after the ten o'clock news they went to bed. At one in the morning, he tied the box into a trash bag and carried it down the alleyway from his mother's house. When he was three blocks from her place, he picked out a trashcan that was already half filled, and tossed the bag into it.

It occurred to him the letters his mother claimed to have in a drawer might have addresses to find the bastard on them. He planned while he waited for morning light, making a mental note to call ahead and give Butch the addresses to check out. He hated the idea of Dorsey getting what was coming to him by someone else's hands, but dead was dead, and he wouldn't harm anyone else with his cowardice and greed.

Freakshow was on the road by ten a.m. He was going to the crib, dropping off the things he'd found and find out if any more information about Dorsey could be found. He would give it three days, if they hadn't found anything more, he planned to hit the road and find the bastard.

*****

"You can come with me, we can get the guys or hire someone to pack the house up. I have to be back in court about Kevin, or I'd find a way to stay to help. I want you to come with me."

They were snuggled together in her big bed, and she had to bite her lip to keep from telling him that she was falling in love with him. He was a grouch, he was oversized and spoiled rotten, and he would always try to be the boss. The only thing holding her back was his lack of offering her anything more than being his fuck buddy, and after their first sexual encounter, it ceased to be casual for her.

She knew he must care something about her because he wouldn't have driven all this way for a piece of ass. Instead of answering him she snuggled in closer to his warmth. She needed more, she needed all of him.

Chapter Twelve

By the time Big Dog and Larry got home to the compound, Butch had relocated just about every one that normally stayed there over night. He'd announced the club was planning to have an old-fashioned camp out week. Something bikers rarely did anymore. They would all go to Big Dog's place and take the kids, making it a family affair. He'd caught a lot of shit from some of the old ladies and wives, but they went with it.

The fluffers and easy rides were told to keep their clothes decent, and he got smacked on the arm by one of them called Cherry. "I ain't no whore that don't know how to act in public, I got kids of my own you know." Yeah, he knew that Cherry knew how to act, that was why she was one of the fluffers, she had a way of sucking a man's cock and balls into tight stiff attention within minutes. She sucked like a vacuum and fucked like a jackhammer. She wanted to be voted in as a house cat, but she had kids, and it wasn't going to happen. She was now eyeballing Poppa for the slot of her old man.

The tag of Big D, as Larry kept calling him, caught on within hours and he was tired as shit, but he and Crazy Charlie and Poppa and Georgie worked in teams of two sweeping the compound and the buildings for explosives. Larry and two Prospects sat at the gate scanning the trees surrounding the drive. The men didn't find any explosives. They found where someone had been smoking cigarettes and stomping them out in the dirt. The suspects were not of the adult variety, considering the wrappers and wads of chewed gum that littered the spot.

They ate cold sandwiches for dinner and washed them down with cold beers. When Charlie and Poppa went out to relieve the guards at the gate, they found Larry slumped over in his chair and one of the Prospects was lying in the dirt. They checked on Larry to see if he was dead or not. Luckily enough, the young man had been tapped on the head, instead of shot or knifed. The gate was open and there was a Prospect missing.

They carried Larry into the main building and yelled for Big Dog and Georgie. They saw what was happening, and ran outside to bring the kid inside. They dropped the boy for Charlie and Poppa to deal with, and went behind the bar to access the small arsenal in a large floor locker. Georgie handed a sawed off twelve gauge pump action to Charlie, and an identical one to Poppa, before arming himself with a double barrel sawed off and a mini Mac with conversion to full auto, with four clips, five if he wanted to include the clip that he'd slapped up into the handle of the gun. Big Dog helped himself to the guns and chose a 1911 colt, and an MP-5 with a night scope, a pistol grip, and collapsible stock, two thirty round clips, and he slapped the locker lid down.

"I'm going out through the flop room window, if it's Dorsey, he'll be expecting us to go out the back or front. He's such a lazy fucker, he won't move far from his rat's nest. I would tell you guys to go to ground in the basement, but you're grown damn men and I want to say, it's been a damn good fuckin' ride. If I don't see you later, I'll see you on the other side with a cold beer waiting for you."

He rolled out onto the grass through the ground level window. It had been a while since the flop rooms were used that most people had forgotten them. They were originally designed for quick exits during the biker wars back in the Fifty's and Sixty's. He stayed on his stomach as he crawled through the grass keeping the night vision scope to his eye and his finger ready to squeeze the trigger. A bike started up in the front and he cautiously looked around the corner of the building.

Three more bikes were at the gate ready to leave, and it puzzled him to see an unfamiliar patch on the back of one of the men trying to hotwire the rat bike. None of the four had a Bastards' personal ride. The bikes had to have been rolled out of the shed in the back. He caught the face of the missing Prospect in the scope, and almost laughed. The little fuckers were trying to start their own group. The patches were crudely drawn, with daggers and guns crossed in the center.

He didn't give a shit about the ragged out bikes, but he couldn't stand a turncoat motherfucker who'd steal from his club. He took careful aim and squeezed the trigger. He watched as the front tire blew and the boys heard the shot. They all ducked and covered their heads. The next shot kicked up the dirt next to two of them, and the boys crawled into the woods.

"You boys can leave under your own steam or you can leave in a box, make your choice, and hurry up about it. My damn finger is getting twitchy." He laid down twenty shots around the spot they were attempting to hide. The boys in the woods were hiding behind trees, but a shot by their side still got them to understand he wasn't fucking with them. A shot came back to his left, and since the boys didn't appear to be armed, he swung the MP-5 toward the direction the shot came from. He saw someone running through the woods, trying to avoid his sights. He tracked the figure, waiting for the man to stop and attempt another shot. The only time the figure hesitated, it was to look over his shoulder, and Big Dog got a clear view of Reeker's desperate face. By the time he turned back to see what the stooges were doing, three bikes were gone and the one with the flat tire sat where it was dropped.

Chances were the only one of the bikes that would start and run for any length of time was the one he'd heard. They used the rat bikes to blow off steam, and fuck around the back field. Most of the tires were bald, and few had front brakes. Those boys might break their own necks, but the theft would still have to be taken seriously. Tiny would have the Prospect's name and home address, or next of kin.

He went to the front door and yelled to the occupants. "Coming in, I need a cold one." He still stayed on the jam side of the door when he turned the knob, just in case one of the men was trigger happy or nervous. "Hey, baby, I'm home," he announced, and walked in the door.

Georgie was laughing so hard, he sounded like he would cough up a lung. Poppa just shook his head and sneered, trying to keep himself from laughing out loud, but the image in his brain from Big Dog's descriptive narration of the skinny assed stooges running down the drive pushing bikes that would cost more to fix than to replace, made him give it up and rumbles of laughter came out of his mouth.

Charlie had no problem picturing the boys hitting the dirt and even speculated whether they had pissed themselves or not when the bullets skimmed the ground around them. Larry was mad and wanted blood. Nothing the men said would console the young man. The twenty-year-old Prospect was awake and had a headache. Every time they laughed he held his head and cringed.

The knowledge that Reeker was trying to start his own club was slightly sobering. Big Dog snapped his fingers and grabbed his phone.

"This is Big Dog, put Wolfman on." He grinned at the men staring open mouthed and bursting to laugh out, but they had to keep quiet. Charlie couldn't help himself, he hit the door running, and the other's followed him, narrowly missing his bent figure as he tried to catch his breath between bursts of laughter. Wolfman was going to have to deal with his former member, and they enjoyed the idea.

They brought the bike back through the gate and padlocked the opening for the night. Poppa and Georgie took the first watch. It was doubtful they would return, but so far they hadn't displayed a great deal of intelligence, so anything was possible.

*****

Freakshow got to the crib before noon. He found Big D in the dining room eating a huge plate of scrambled eggs. He grinned at the man who had become his friend. "You've got Larry in the kitchen right? He cooks a mean egg, but don't let him near a chicken, trust me."

He went to the coffeemaker and poured a cup of the grayish black liquid that no amount of creamer would lighten the color. He walked back to the table and started talking. The big man only interrupted to make certain points clear in his understanding before nodding for him to continue. He was more interested in the notebooks than the bag of gold. The solution of tossing the trophy box was a good one and Big D told him so. "I told my mom to go visit my aunt, Stephanie, in Florida for the winter. I stayed the extra hours to make sure she got on that plane. I bought her a new cell phone with a new number, and gave her a few dollars to play with at the reservation casinos while she's there.

"I want to have permission to hunt Dorsey. I let him go once, it wasn't on purpose, but still, someone has to take care of business. If he finds out that Future isn't dead. He will be back. Her reappearance fucked up his world. Those notebooks would make some good blackmail. You do what you want with them. I would burn them, at least the ones that pertain to the Bastards. I have a few leads, and I know what he looks like without the scruff and bike. I can keep in touch, but I want sanctioned in case I get the opportunity."

Big D told him to get some shuteye. "I need to think about this for a bit. I'll let you know what my decision is tonight." With nothing else to say to convince the man, he followed the order to get some sleep.

*****

Future stared at the detective. "You found what? I'm sorry, I must be dreaming. Did you really say that you found four bodies in the walls of the tunnel?"

Three days after the fire she'd been called into the police station to give her statement formally. Everything seemed routine until a guy who introduced himself as Lt. Vince Bellows asked her to step into this room. It was such a small room that she wondered what the hell was going on and started to ask him what this was about, when he ordered her to sit down. Before she knew what was happening, she was sitting and the detective was asking her who the bodies in the tunnel were.

"No, Miss Smith, I assure you I am not joking, and you're not dreaming. The Fire Marshall was determining the cause of the explosion, and found two bodies. Didn't you notice the heavy equipment digging around in the parking lot between the bar and your residence? So far there have been four bodies and we anticipate there will be more. Since you have been the owner of record for almost three years, and you told the officer on duty the night of the explosion that you had gone through the tunnel minutes before the place blew up, I'm sure you can understand why I have to ask you these questions."

"I bought a place with dead bodies buried in concrete walls? Mr. Brennbury never disclosed he had dead people in the walls. He said he needed to retire because he was tired of the cold winters and he wanted to travel to Florida and Arizona in the wintertime. He is such a nice old man. He accepted my offer even though it was really low, and he even holds the mortgage. Why would he do that if he was a murderer? I send him the payments every month." She looked at the detective and shook her head. This could not be happening. "I have no idea what to say to this. I get my building blown up, and if that's not bad enough, I have four or more bodies that are dead, and what am I supposed to do with dead people? The insurance company is already giving me shit about paying to rebuild. My mother is supposed to be coming to stay with me because she's tired of her old man's shit and…damn, just damn."

The detective got up and left the room, and Future took the time to compose her thoughts. She had been tested many times. The miserable childhood with Merlin, her disastrous marriage to Bert. The three weeks of torture and years of feeling so broken she often wondered why she hadn't given up. The humiliation of showing her scars to six men. The certainty the old President of the Chiefs was, in all probability, her sperm donor, the worry for her mother, the building blowing up, and now dead people?

The detective came back into the room and handed her a bottle of water. "I have to tell you, I don't believe you are a murderess. The thing is, we have to find your Mr. Brennbury. We need any information that you can give us, and I don't want to give you even more grief, but you might as well hear it now. We have to take the house down to make sure all of the bodies have been found. I asked the captain, and he said you can have three days to get your personal stuff and any furnishings that you think you might need to furnish another place to live."

"There's no way I can get everything out of that house in three days. I don't have a place to put it, and it is the only home I have, how can you expect me to just leave all of those antiques? If I lose the bar and the house, I'll still owe the mortgage and I'll probably have to sell the furniture to pay the payments. The insurance company won't pay for another house if you tear mine down, dammit. I need to call a lawyer."

She was still muttering about credit scores and insurance companies when he escorted her out of the building.

That night, she took the Heritage out and burned a tank of gas trying to clear her head. She kept thinking about the things she'd said to the detective and cringed. She had sounded like a brainless fool. To be fair, she'd felt that way at the time too. She needed help, and while she hated to admit it, she needed to hear Hugh's voice. Maybe he could offer some advice, or one of those big shoulders to rest her head on. It would be nice to have someone to care once in a while. Always being strong when you know you're not as tough as you act got old quick.

It was almost midnight when she called to tell him what happened. She did her best to keep the rising panic from choking her as she spoke. "They acted like I was the one that buried the damn bodies in concrete."

He snapped at her, "What the fuck, Future, why didn't you call Hall and Early? They would be right there, and you never go back into that place without an attorney with you again. You call them in the morning, or I will if you need me to." She began to feel better. A bit dumbassed for not remembering the law firm's name the Bastards used when they needed representation.

"Hugh, I have had it up to my eyeballs in bullshit here. Now I have three days to clean the house out before they begin to tear it down. You've been here, the place is filled with antiques from the last hundred years or more. Detective Bellows told me to take what I needed if I couldn't get everything out in the three days. They handed me a court order on my way out of the police station.

"So unless the lawyers have a house for me to furnish with Italian vases and massive pieces of furniture like my bed, they can't help me with that. I have racked my brain to try to figure out why Mr. Brennbury left all of this stuff behind. He told me that he didn't need it, and that it was mine to deal with now on the night he came and showed me the tunnel.

"The truth is that I have no idea if I should call an antiques dealer, or a moving company. I don't know many people around here, I've been too damn busy for morning coffee with the neighbors. Sorry to be unloading all of my shit on you like this, I guess I just needed to vent, to tell someone who might give a damn, you know? Since you've been here I mean." She had to get her head on straight or she was going to break down and beg him to come and help her. She wasn't sure either of them was ready for that. He hadn't seemed to have any problem riding off and away from her, and she wasn't wired to beg him to stay if he didn't want to be there.

His, "Alright, this is what I think you should do. In the morning at nine o'clock, call Hall and Early, I'll text you their number. Start packing up what you can, and I'll send a few people to help move the heavy stuff. You can store it at the farmhouse, there's almost no furniture in it yet, and the place is massive, so you can stay there too. It will give you time to decide what you want to do, without a specific timetable."

He promised to talk to her mother, "Although Merlin has been pretty scarce lately. He was telling Georgie that he was thinking about heading to Colorado. They've legalized weed there and anyone that knows him knows he would be all over that. So she might not have to leave the cabin if she doesn't want to. She's been a big help to me with Kevin, he told me she said he could call her Nana, like a real grandma, without all the messy family stuff."

They said goodnight, with him promising to push the guys out the door at first light, and she promised to try to remain calm and call the Suits.

The very idea that her fluffy brained mother was essentially adopting a grandkid was mind blowing.

To allow the kid to call her Nana, that was even more of a surprise. All of her life, she'd been instructed to call her parents by their first names. Maybe the old girl was finally accepting her age. She didn't want to think about it, but she put the information in a small corner of her mind for later examination. Right now, she needed to get her ass in gear and her head where it belonged. Her pity party was over with, and she was ready for tomorrow.

Chapter Thirteen

Matthew Douglas and Larry Watson left the compound wearing their colors and in a couple of days, they'd take them off until they were in neutral territory again. They couldn't fly the Bastards logo in another group's territory without starting an incident and a matter of respect the men understood. Big D refused to allow Show to go on his own. If he was going to sanction the hunt, he wanted a witness, and someone to have his back. Since Larry had appeared to attach himself at the hip to Show, they were now partners in the hunt.

*****

When Big Dog got to the farm, it was a matter of dodging kids and scooters. He found his usual go-to guys and began to explain what Future had gotten herself into. Knight and Demon walked into the conversation a few minutes after he'd begun to tell the men the story, and they got caught up quick. Big Dog waited for the laughter to calm down as it rolled through the men, who'd already heard about the cement fillers in the tunnel.

Demon didn't laugh. He was still pissed that Knight had gotten a piece of that ass of hers. Big Dog didn't even think about him when he called for backup. What kind of friendship was that? They'd shared bitches before with no one getting hurt.

The thought the woman was a walking disaster made him wonder how she could walk and chew gum at the same time without falling into a sinkhole. "That woman could have spent her life in one room with no windows and only a jailer, and trouble would find her. If she has this ESP stuff, why can't she know what's going to happen and stop it then?"

Big Dog didn't like the attitude or the tone, but he let it slide for now, and explained the problem with people like Future. "The way it was explained to me is that most people with her talent can't see their own future. Many of them can't see a loved one's future either, emotion gets in the way and they want to impose their own feelings in the mix or some such shit. I know she has a form of sight, and if you doubt her abilities, I suggest you shake her hand one time to put your mind at rest. Just remember, if you ask her, she will tell you what she sees. So I would be careful to do it privately if I were you. The Chiefs old leader was called the Medicine Man, not for his heritage, more from his love of pills and smoke. He had the same talent, but I think it was stronger in him than what she has."

"Okay, she can't see her own future, and she can only see certain people, it seems kind of convenient to me, but who am I to say right? Okay, what do we need to do for her now? The psychotic bitch has your cock stuck in her cunt, and you want us all to come to her defense. It's not like the rest of us get to fuck her, but even with nothing in it for us we're going to—" His words were cut short when Knight belted him in the jaw with his fist, and the fight was on.

Knight was an inch shorter than Demon, but he was meaner. The man was normally very easy going, but this wasn't a normal type of thing.

144

They'd been in a few fistfights before, but the fights were almost always for personal reasons. Strangely enough, this one was different. There were no grins and verbal taunts between the best friends. The combat was strictly intent to damage each other.

This fight would have epic results if something wasn't done to stop it before one of them seriously hurt the other one. Big Dog weighed in on the fun. He was four inches taller than Demon and when the President stepped in front of Knight to take the punch that had already been thrown, it landed on the big man's shoulder, skimming it, and the momentum behind the punch that didn't connect properly, caused Demon to tilt too far forward to avoid the sledgehammer fist to his gut. The open hand swat to the side of his face, as he was bent over, landed his ass in the dirt.

Knight did not get away easy either. His feet were swept out from under him as he headed for Demon. The hammer fist connected to his jaw, and it was lights out for him.

Demon should have stayed down, Big Dog grabbed the redheaded brawler, and punched him in the gut hard enough to double the big man over, and his fists slugged one side of his jaw and then the other before he allowed Demon to drop to his knees, gasping for breath and gave him a shove backwards into the dirt. He stayed down this time. It was probably the smartest thing he'd done all day.

"The next time you got something to say about Future, be a fucking man and say it to me, don't try to make her out to be the trouble here in front of the rest of the men. I'm pretty sure I know what started this and you two son-of-a-bitches are on my shit list. Get his ass out of here before I kill you both." Big Dog was so mad he wanted to kick their asses over the entire field. He picked up a heavy rock and threw it at another one to vent his ire on. The resulting shrapnel of small quartz stones made everyone hold their arms up to protect their faces, as it shot over the circle they all sat in.

"If anyone else has something to say about Future, now is the time to say it. Speak up now, because the next time a motherfucker starts making accusations, he'd better be spewing facts, not jealous shit out of his pie hole. The woman has done nothing to harm any of us as far as I have seen or heard. Without her we would still be snipping ground with the Breed instead of talking affiliation. If it's any of your business, yes I have fucked her, more than once, and I plan to again as soon as I can get her to stand still for a few minutes so I can get my prick in her. If you object to it, fuck you." He waited, looking around the circle of amused faces. "While you're laughing, I plan to offer her a more permanent position, so if you have any objections, now is the time." No one spoke up, the grins remained. It seemed that Demon and Knight hadn't been the only assholes making a fool of themselves. That damn woman had gotten under all their skin.

"I asked for volunteers, it was a request, not an order."

Kevin came running around the building with his toy gun and several girls were chasing him, he was out of sponge bullets and he saw Big Dog and made a beeline toward his safety net. "Quick, hide

146

me, they want blood." He went behind the tall man's legs and held on, dropping his gun in the dirt so he could wrap his bony little arms around one of his thighs. "I didn't do nuthin', they just started chasing me."

Two of the bolder girls in the pack of five kept coming for him and Big Dog held up his hand when they were about four feet from their intended goal. "Okay, girls, I'm all for women's lib and all, but he is five, and it looks like you've already smacked him a few times. What has you all ready to smack him again?"

A cute little girl with brown curls and narrowed blue eyes huffed and folded her arms across her chest. The little blonde with straight hair to her butt, and snapping blue eyes, scowled at him, and pointed at Kevin. "He took our fashion dolls and shot them. He lined them up on the rail where they drain the coolers, and he shot them with his gun, and they landed in the mud." The little pissed off female took a long-suffering deep breath and continued her prosecution. "Jasper Wright's dogs thought it was fun to grab our dolls and chew them into pieces when they fought over them."

The little brunette was nodding her head and piped up with, "We got Jasper, he is in the mud, and he better stay there until we get back with Kevin." By then, the other three girls had moved forward, and they were all bobbing their heads.

He had a choice here, he could be the kid's hero, and save his little ass from the physical wrath of the herd of girls, or he could give in to the impulse and turn him over to take his just deserts. He pulled

Kevin lose from his leg and squatted down to talk to him closer to his level. "Did you take the dolls?" Kevin nodded and hung his head. "Okay, this is what you will do." He turned to the girls and made Kevin face them too.

"On Friday, you ladies meet Kevin and Jasper in front of the house here, and I will drive you to the store. Kevin and Jasper will accompany you as you each find a doll to replace the ones that have been ruined. Kevin will pay for them from his birthday money. Jasper will buy leashes for his dogs and begin training them or he won't be able to bring them here again. And since Kevin is my son, I might find time to take you to the place with the mouse thing and all of the games." He looked from girl to girl and they were staring at him open mouthed at first. The head bobbing started again, and he told them to go let Jasper get out of the mud.

They took off running, and he pulled an unhappy Kevin around to stand in front of him. "What you did was funny for you right? But what you did affected other people too, and since you are the only one who didn't get hurt from what you started, you get to pay your share of the hurt, with your money. Our actions always have to be thought out before we do something to other people, or we pay for it. You are also going to start doing more chores, like taking the trash out and I'm taking your gun until you can be more responsible. Go put it in the garage on the workbench, and leave the girls alone. If you do something like this again, I'll have to let them take you, those two girls scared me."

148

He hated to face the men, it seemed it was his day to deal with badly behaving males that were close to him. He turned to go back to face the laughs, and stopped in surprise to see Charlie with his arm around Ms. Prissy Pants, the child advocate, staring at him. Only this wasn't the uptight prune lipped female he remembered. This woman had a bit of make-up on, and wore jeans and a tank top with a hog depicted in caricature.

She had to have seen Kevin and his fan club. Why not? The only reason he wasn't on his bike right this minute headed to Future was that woman. He had to show up in court in the morning to defend his parenting skills and now she saw what a fuck up he was up close and personal. What the hell was Charlie thinking to bring her here? He was gonna have to call Early and disturb his Sunday with this. *Fuck, just fuck.*

Seth and Tarzan came up to him and promised to help Future move her things. "She's a decent sort, and it'll piss off Demon, that's good enough for me." Seth was being wordy in that sentence. He liked to grunt and nod instead of talk to communicate. Tiny and his woman, Lila, offered to take the box truck and help too.

*****

She stood in the middle of the attic, and had no idea where to start on all of the boxes and trunks. She had the largest rental van they would rent to her without a CDL license, sitting in her driveway. She decided to pack it all in the truck and hopefully Hugh had a lot of room in his house and maybe if she was lucky, he had an outbuilding. She opened a trunk that looked like it had been all around the world with all of the stickers decorating the thing. She found vintage dresses and small rolls of cloth with a pearl necklace and earrings in the rolled cloth, shoes to match and long white gloves to complete the outfit. The jewelry was stuffed in the shoes; Emeralds, Amethysts, and Jade stones to color coordinate with each outfit, blew her mind. For the first time in her life, she wanted to wear a dress.

Another trunk contained men's suits. Shiny silk shirts, and pinstriped suits, with two pair of leather shoes, that had the familiar rolled cloth, it contained watches and tiepins. One had a man's pinky ring was imbedded with what she would swear was a dime sized diamond. She closed the trunks and left the attic, wondering what the nice old man had been doing here in the dying neighborhood. There was more than enough wealth here to allow him to live in luxury for the rest of his life and still have enough to keep the local dog shelter in cash for a year or two.

The attorneys had been there that morning, and told her that if she could, it would be best to comply with the court order. As the handsome Jethro Hall told her, "The place is considered a crime scene, they didn't have to be nice about it and give you more than twenty-four hours. Take what you can get out and be happy."

The police had been there and taken hundreds of photographs and videos. They said it was routine, but she knew they were carefully sifting through stolen property lists. They must have found another body this morning, because when she looked out of her back door, the black and gold SUV was there, and people were running around the spot that had just been opened in the parking lot.

At four o'clock in the afternoon, she was carrying another box of unknown stuff from the attic to put in the trailer, when a thunderous noise could be heard. She knew that sound. Hugh had promised to send a few guys, but this was more than a few. She came around the rental truck and was happy to see ten hogs pulling in front of the house. She recognized Seth and Georgie, and she remembered seeing the chubby guy that gave her shit the first day she went back to the crib. Tarzan let out a whoop when he saw her, and even Needles had come. Tilly, the uncrowned queen of the club's bitches, brought Janice aka Juicy with her. Even Harlow had come, she was riding on Tarzan's bitch pad, and Harlow never went out of her way for anyone that Future could remember.

Harlow, it seemed, had a personal agenda, and she walked right up to Future and held out her hand. "Here's the deal, you tell me what I want to know, and I help you."

Future took the offered hand and could feel that underneath the sarcastic bitch persona, Harlow was actually frightened. She was three months pregnant and didn't remember who the father was. She'd been having sex with both men, sometimes at the same time. Technically either man could be the father of the child, except there were two children, one had blue eyes like her mother, and the boy had brown eyes. She could see their auras and Harlow

151

was in for some fun when the twins got together with their fathers. "I would say both men, one child has brown eyes and one has blue eyes. Your eyes are hazel. Seth and Tarzan are lucky men.

"Now, since I know your secret, you can pack up the dishes in the hutch and kitchen if you want, one of the guys can carry them out for you."

She ended up directing the packing, and even paid for rooms at the motel along the highway. When Tiny and his old lady showed up with the box truck, they loaded the cases of liquor into it, and as much of the fragile stuff as they could fit in the space that surprisingly held more than it was first thought to hold.

She ordered takeout pizza and gave her truck keys to Janice for a beer run. She had plenty of soft drinks, but the beer kegs had been destroyed in the fire.

The next morning, everyone was back to help and there was only her room and the basement to get packed and on the truck.

Detective Bellows and a uniform stopped by to check on the progress of the move, and everyone knew he was curious as to who the bikes in front of the house belonged to. Future didn't bother to introduce any of the group to him except Janice and Tilly. The women amused themselves flirting with the detective and his colleague for a short time, and started hauling boxes to the truck.

A shout from the basement door got everyone in the house's attention. Georgie and one of the Prospects came upstairs at a fact clip, with a box. George wasted no time dropping the thing on the counter and stepped away from it. The Prospect ran to the back door and hurled his guts out. Future reached to pull the flap back and stopped her hand in midair. "Are you fucking kidding me? Entire bodies weren't enough? There's heads too?"

She narrowed her eyes and walked over to Detective Bellows and touched his cheek for the few seconds it took him to jerk away from her touch. "You knew, you knew the heads were missing from those bodies, and you didn't say anything to me about it. Is there anything else you neglected to tell me? Because I am doing my best to not go psychic bitch on you right now."

Bellows and the uniform called in the discovery and headed down the basement stairs with the box.

Future's room was now empty, all of the rooms were cleared out down to the rugs that had been on the floors. Every closet and loose board in the floors had been checked out to make certain they'd missed nothing. She left the floor safe open after taking her hard earned cash out of it. A couple of the more enterprising men had pulled the fountain from the spot in the back yard and loaded it, and the lawn ornaments that weren't religious symbols, were stowed in the back too.

Before everyone left, Future handed out money to each of the people who'd come to help. She told them to keep it, they still had to buy gas and stay another night in a hotel along the drive back. Not to mention eating would cost a bit more. They started leaving soon after. She stood next to her truck where the Heritage was strapped down to keep it from falling during the drive to Hugh's place. She wanted to walk through the house one more time, but the police had their tape up and uniforms were every ten feet or so. The place was now a death house as far as she was concerned. The heads cinched that for her. She waved to the detective as she started down the street. A new chapter in an old place waited, and the idea made her nervous.

She caught up with Tiny and Lila at the motel that night. Tarzan had decided to sleep in the truck since Harlow was riding with him. And most of the others either stayed elsewhere, or continued on toward home.

She lectured herself most of the way to the farmhouse. She had to stop thinking of Big Dog as Hugh. He had been there for her when she felt like a lost cause, but she'd sacrificed her pride to further the Bastards agenda too. If she was honest with herself, she could have found someone in the club that was good with a rifle, and paid them to take out the fuckers that had caused her to go to ground and lick her wounds. The beatings and torture had been severe, and she'd been through hell. Maybe she should have taken retribution sooner. One thing she did know, the time away from the family and the group had changed her. She no longer had the ability to allow someone to order her around like the trick pony that she'd often compared herself to. She had grown into her own while she was in her self-imposed absence. She was ready to acknowledge her accomplishments, and for the first time, she actually liked who she'd become.

It had taken caring people to help her come to the notion, and she wanted to hug Matthew for repairing her ravaged skin. She wanted to kiss Big Dog for being a horny Bastard with a screwed up sense of beauty. The text of a picture of his penis this morning made her grin. The caption: He Misses You, was as close to romance that she might get from him, but if he was offering more at some time in the near future, she would be taking him up on it.

She followed the box truck down the driveway to the farmhouse. When she parked her truck in front of the garage, and got out to stretch her legs, she stared at the house. It was built in the Victorian style with a tower and huge wraparound porch. The house was certainly huge as Big Dog had said it was. Toy trucks and a small bicycle laid on its side in the yard. The place was a house, not a cabin, or a duplex. It screamed sanctuary and home. She loved it.

The big rental truck pulled up beside the box truck and Tarzan got out. There was no sign of Harlow, but he might have dropped her off before coming there.

The bikes showed up shortly after the truck did, and the process of unloading everything began. Most of the boxes and trunks were offloaded into the pole barn so Future could go through them later, and not mess up the house with all of the clutter and dust. The dining room table and chairs looked like they belonged in the house and so did the chests of drawers, wardrobes, and the brocade fireside chairs. The beds were put in the pole barn for now.

Charlie let them in, saying Big Dog had to be in court again today, but he should be back shortly. The old man kept saying that he remembered a lot of this stuff from his childhood, and Georgie teased him about his age. That didn't get a rise from the victim, so Georgie asked him how his woman was doing, "Is she ready to dump your old ass for a younger one like me." Got the reaction he hoped for, and they traded insults for the next hour.

The trucks were unloaded except for the liquor and wine. Future told Tiny to take it to the clubhouse if he thought the club would want it. She pulled two cases of whisky and two cases of wine out of the truck to have at the house. "I just got the delivery two days before the fire and I'm glad that something survived. Even if it's a thousand dollars worth of whiskey and wine."

Chapter Fourteen

Tarzan took the rental back and Butch drove behind him to give him a ride home. Big Dog texted a message telling her to make herself at home, he would be coming home later than he thought. So she filled the deep old clawfoot tub with hot water and soaked until she was pruny. She looked through the fridge and got a beer and a thick ham sandwich, before turning out the lights and going into the small room with the curved couch and a large screen TV.

She was asleep before the sandwich and beer were half gone. That's where Hugh found her when he got home. He'd meant to be here when she pulled in the driveway, but the paperwork on his adoption of Kevin had to be dealt with, and he stopped by Selma Pearson's office to thank her. He'd run into Cliff Abbot, one of the members of the Bastards, and had to buy the brother a meal and a few beers in town. The poor fucker was so riddled with cancer the doctor's thought it was linked to the pesticides that Cliff used in his exterminating business. He had an electric wheelchair that was his only transportation now, and he was bored. So Big Dog spent a few hours with him to let him know he wasn't forgotten by the group.

The added plus to caring about Cliff was the man knew everything that went on in town. He wanted his brothers to know about the new gang of bikers that were said to be real hardcore. Sheriff Lorne Iszcabiec sat with a deputy behind the partition in the diner, and Cliff gave Big Dog the "someone's listening" sign, when he brought up the subject.

"You know, Big Dog, this new group are said to make the Breed look like a bunch of rah-rah girls. They have a patch they say Satan inspired too. It is a sword and some kind of carbine crossed in the middle and all kinds of medieval weapons in the outside of the circle." Cliff paused for a moment, and from the way he seemed to be trying to compose himself without laughing, Big Dog knew it was going to be a good one. He wasn't disappointed.

"They call themselves, Satan's Hammer MC, and they are spreading the reputation they have killed and stolen their way up the coast in California and coming this way. Yep, you boys had better watch out, they plan to take over the territory here real soon."

It was his turn to try to compose himself without laughing out loud, he couldn't help the choking sounds from escaping, there was no way he would disclose what he knew about the "New Gang". He drank down half a beer and finally could say a few words without giggling like a schoolgirl. "Well, Cliff, you know how we hate all the fighting and shit that comes with being a MC group. If they show up, we'll just call the sheriff and his men to deal with an outlaw group like that. We're taxpayers and expect to be protected and served just like any other citizen in this county." There was already a group called Satan's Hammer in Kentucky and Tennessee. It would be interesting to see the real deal meet up with the bottom feeders.

The sound of glass breaking on the other side of the partition gave the two of them satisfaction. They loved to pull the arrogant sheriff's chain, and the man was too damn dumb to realize it. This was a routine for Cliff and Big Dog, it gave Cliff some form of entertainment, and he enjoyed feeding half assed shit like this to the sheriff who thought he was being sneaky. If the dumb bastard would come to him and ask, he might get more cooperation, but there was no chance of that happening, the man would rather be shot by his own gun than ask for help.

When they left the diner, Big Dog explained the situation to Cliff, and they both laughed until tears rolled down their cheeks. It had been worth the time Big Dog took with Cliff. As soon as he was on his bike, and out of town, he opened the hog up and drove. He didn't need to be psychic to know that Cliff didn't have much time left on this earth. That might be the last time they got the privilege to fuck with the sheriff, and it made him sad.

Now that he was home and watching Future as she slept, he knew where they were headed. Her being here was proof enough that she'd learned to trust him. That pussy bike of hers was parked in his garage, and she was in a tank top and shorts, asleep in front of the TV. She looked like she was at home, and he planned to keep it that way.

He grinned, Kevin was with Muffy, and he had a beautiful sexy woman in the house. It was time to take advantage of the situation.

Future woke up to sunshine blazing through the sheer curtains in the master bedroom. She stretched her legs and felt the burn in her muscles from last night's activities. Hugh had gone out of his way to make an impression, and he succeeded. Her nipples hardened as she remembered his determination to turn her into one big nerve of pleasure. She learned to appreciate his stamina for making love. Last night couldn't be described as screwing, it was too raw and beautiful to be reduced to something so impersonal. She'd tried to return the pleasures he gave her and hope she succeeded as well as he did for her.

She sat up and had to stare at the big beautiful man lying next to her hip, with his forearm over his eyes, and his bulging muscles on display in the sunlight. She felt so much love in her heart for him at this moment that she had to tell him. She climbed on top of him and began kissing his wide chest. His nipples were in her way, so they were nibbled on in turn as she made her way up his whiskered neck and chin to his lips. She felt his prick wake from its slumber and it stretched under the lips of her wet flesh. She adjusted her hips to allow it to keep growing while penetrating her pussy. This fullness was what she needed this morning, and with a last lick on his lips, she sat up and began to ride his hips. "Good morning, sunshine, I hope you don't mind, but I need this to start my day. By the way, I want to say I love you before I get too far out of my head to say it and you'd know I mean it." She leaned up, and looked down to where his thick prick was disappearing into her body, causing her to speed up her efforts to pleasure both of them.

She found herself flat on her back with his body buried deep and his lips crushing hers. His thumb was pinching her unprotected clit and she fell into a pleasure so deep she saw colors burst in her mind, vivid colors, and muscle tightening physical pleasure.

He hadn't told her he loved her, and she was happy he didn't try to say words he didn't mean. She hoped her confession didn't make him feel like she wanted to trap him into declaring his undying love or anything like that. It would be nice to know she wasn't in the emotional aspect of the relationship by herself though.

They got up and showered together. The laughter she brought to his life was filling a big hole he hadn't known was there. He wasn't a fancy talker, and maybe she could do better, but he wasn't going to wait much longer to let her know that she had a place in his heart. She said she loved him and he had every intention of holding her to it.

"How about we go for a ride, I have a place that I love to go to once in a while, you can see the whole valley from my spot." He took the towel from her body and began to rub her wet hair with one hand as his other hand skimmed over her silky skin. "I love your skin, it's so silky and smooth that my fingers itch to explore every inch of you." He dropped the towel onto the side of the sink and began kissing her lips, working his way down her neck, and enjoying the way goose bumps formed on her soft shoulders.

His mouth found her nipple and his hands grabbed the backs of her knees, lifting her onto the vanity top. When he dropped to his knees with his head between her thighs, Future giggled from the feel of his whiskers tickling the sensitive nerve endings under the sweep of his beard. She held onto the counter with one hand and grabbed a handful of his wet hair with the other, "Oh yes, I love the way you do that, please, yes." His tongue worked its magic and twirled over her clit and then dipped inside of her welcoming body. He stuck two fingers inside of her pussy and sucked strongly on her hard clit, tonguing it while the vacuum of his mouth pulled the shy muscle up and stiff, "God, Hugh, oh that's so good, I'm ready to come." She could feel the spasms beginning deep inside of her cunt, and began to move her hips, causing the scrape of his teeth over her exposed clit. "Oh fuck yes." She was tumbling over the cliff and enjoying the fall, when he stood and slammed his thick cock deep. Her nails scored his shoulders as she cried out her love for him and for the way he fucked her.

He got a kick in the heart each time he heard those words from her lips. His heart was pounding and he could no more stop fucking her tight pussy than he could stop the words "Mine, this is mine, no fucking one else's" from spilling from between his gritted teeth, as the come shot from his prick. His arms came around her and they stayed in that position until their breathing began to slow down. He helped her down from the counter, and they cleaned up with a quick rinse with the showerhead before getting dressed, pulling denim over damp skin, and tangling her bra when he tried to help her put the damn thing on.

He brought his bike around front. She locked the door and hopped on behind him. She never hesitated this time, her hands held on to his belt as he accelerated down the driveway and onto the road. He pulled the bike onto a dirt two track, and they rode up into the hills of the forest. When they finally stopped at the spot he loved to come to, she could see why it held so much appeal.

"It's beautiful here." Seeing nothing but the colors of the forest for miles surrounding them, made her realize he was sharing something more than just his home and body with her. "You love me, I know you love me or we wouldn't be here, and if the words never leave your lips, I'll always know, because this is your special place." She went to him and pulled his head down for her kiss, "I love you, and thank you for bringing me here."

He wrapped her in his arms with her back to his front, and felt his prick begin to stir. "You have a place right here, in my arms. You have no idea how strong and invincible I feel when you say my name, or the way you fall apart when you come as I'm deep inside of you. You smile and I get hard. Damn, woman, when you hurt, I want to kill what or who hurt you. Hearing you tell me that you love me, you have no clue how that made me feel. It is indescribable.

"Fuck it all, not going to fight it. I want you in my home, smiling at me till it hurts like a bitch until I've got you under me screaming my name, and squeezing the come from my cock. I want to see

163

you in my kitchen teaching Kevin to make burgers, or doing mom shit with him. He is my nephew, my sister was a drug addict, but you know that already don't you? We are a packaged deal, if you decide to take us on, which I have every intention of making you want to stay, 'cause I refuse to let you go. And I promise you will never regret one day of it."

She turned in his arms and shared a kiss that left them both yanking at each other's clothing, and when Hugh pulled her to his bike and arranged her lying over the gas tank, straddling the seat, he buried his cock deep into her wet pussy.

The gas cap was between her shoulder blades and pushed her breasts up, making it convenient for his hands to play with her large mounds. He twisted the rings in her nipples and groaned, "I fuckin' love to see these all tight and ready for my hands." He had to bow his back to lean down and take the tender nub into his mouth, but that didn't slow down her hips from working his cock as deep as she could inside of her hot tunnel.

Only the birds and woodland creatures witnessed the way she screamed low between her teeth as she came, and the way the man that had given her such pleasure stared at her when her eyes closed. Her hips jerked faster against his as he growled the words she thought she would never hear leave his lips as he filled her wet depths with his come. "I love you. God, woman, you make me smile inside, and you fucking know it."

She smiled inside herself with the knowledge she alone would be the only one to see and hear this softer side of this man. And she knew she would cherish every tender moment she shared with him.

*****

The club was full of Sunday morning hungry people. As Big Dog led her into the lounge with their plates, Kevin ran over to get a hug, and stared at Future for quite a while as he sat next to his new dad. He leaned over and whispered something in his father's ear, and got a shrug, before Big Dog stood and took the child's hand in his. "We'll be back in a few minutes."

She finished her coffee and was about to gather the plates and mugs when they came back. Kevin stopped in front of her and said, "He is my new dad you know." She nodded solemnly. Big Dog held a new leather cut out to her, and she stood to take it. He shook his head and stepped up close, holding the vest for her to put on. It was his idea of asking her to be his old lady. Wearing it was her yes answer. When he went down on his knee, she was shocked.

"Marry me." He didn't ask, it came out as more of a demand, but she didn't care, she knocked him on his ass when she tackled him, landing on his gut, kissing his lips, as everyone was laughing. She didn't notice the jeweled eyes of the skeleton in the logo that he'd customized himself.

*****

The party that followed that night was great, and Demon wove his way to the newly engaged couple that was standing around, talking to people. He plopped down on his knees and grabbed her hips in his hands before leaning over and placing a loud smacking kiss on the cheek of her ass. He got up,

165

nodded to Big Dog, and went to the bar. The catcalls and laughter made him bow and raise his glass, "To you, my lady, may you continue to make my friend smile. Be good to each other."

He made his way to the back rooms to take a quick nap, but could only stare in shock, until he was told to "Either join in or get the fuck out." He shook his head and clicked the button on the door handle so any unsuspecting person checking the rooms wouldn't see what he'd just seen. He went back to the party and ordered a well deserved whiskey in his book. He quickly downed the first one and pushed his glass toward the bartender to refill it. He walked over to the small crowd of people consisting of Knight, Big Dog, and Needles, standing next to Tarzan.

Big Dog found the expression on Demon's face odd. He hadn't planned to ask, but the blank faced look was so curious that he had to know what was going on. He clapped Demon on the shoulder, "Hey, buddy, what's got you looking like a virgin on his wedding night?"

Demon finished his drink. "You don't want to know exactly what I just saw, man, trust me on that. I go to lay down for a few and opened the backroom door, fucking Charlie has a woman." He turned back to the bar and grabbed the beer that Joey had put there for Knight. "I need to get drunk, too fuckin' drunk to want to get laid. That cockblocking old bastard, first the hot piece of tail waitress, and now I don't know who he has back there with him. That old son-of-a-bitch can get women, I haven't had one in a damned week. Now, I need eye bleach, the sight of his old ass... Fuck. I can't even think of that." He shuddered and knocked back the shot.

Hugh had no response for the poor bastard, he slapped him on the back again and leaned down to Future, quietly asking her if she felt like having him be good to her right now, and she laughingly nodded as he pulled her through the crowd, through the back door and into the duplex. He planned to be good to her later when they got home too. For now, the duplex would do.

Epilogue

Knight watched Big Dog haul his woman over his shoulder and head into the dark. Kevin had gone home with Muffy, his new Nana, Demon was sitting in the corner drinking himself into oblivion. Not that he blamed him after what he witnessed.

He never thought he'd be jealous to see a man voluntarily lock down like Big Dog just did today. He liked his job of riding between clubs and busting heads where it was needed. Some of the things he'd done as a Nomad for the Bastards was boring as hell, others were the adrenalin for his dark side. It was time he started earning his keep. There was a couple of threats to the club on the loose, and it was his job to eliminate those threats. Normally, he would have his friend with him on a hunt, but Demon wasn't the same man he'd been—or maybe it was him who had changed.

He finished his beer and headed for the door. He needed to get some sleep, and be ready to ride in the morning.

About the Author

Ryder Dane

I write about MC Groups aka Biker Books, because I've lived with Motorcycles my entire life. It made me smile when a reviewing reader said that there was a realistic feel to my writing! Having been an "Old Lady" since I was 19 gives me the advantage of using a few real details of MC life. I am very happy to bring readers my stories and having them invest in my characters' lives.

Website: Ryderdane.com

Books by Ryder Dane

Big Dog (Burning Bastards MC Book 1)
Nomad's Fall (Burning Bastards MC Book 2)
Charlie's Heart (Burning Bastards MC Series Book 3)

Sanctuary Within the Breed
(Lucifer's Breed MC Book 1)
Integrity Has No Bounds (Lucifer's Breed Book 2)
Starting Over (Lucifer's Breed Book 3)